# Under the Stars

Katherine Taylor

For Lee,

Thank you for all your support and keeping me motivated.

# Chapter 1

"What do you think they're fighting about this time?" Liam asked with a sigh as his uninterested older brother searched through the contacts in his phone for someone to hang out with that evening. Liam didn't bother taking his phone out, he only really had it for emergencies.

"Could be anything," Jeremy replied without looking up. The two brothers were leant against the small brick wall at the bottom of the driveway, their usual spot where they could avoid hearing their parents scream at each other.

Finally, Jeremy put his phone away into his jeans pocket and sighed in defeat. "No-one's around tonight," he said as he stood up straight. "Did you want to come with me to that amusement park outside of town?"

Silence thickened the air between them as they walked slowly up the side of the main road to the entrance of the amusement park. The car park was already full and they could hear the excited screams of the families inside.

The two brothers joined the short line as it moved quickly towards the entrance. Liam caught a few of the girls in the line throwing Jeremy admiring glances, and maybe even him too. He blushed, wondering if they thought the two brothers were twins. Jeremy was six years older than Liam, but their faces were almost identical and they were a similar height now that Liam had gone through his growth spurt, making him the tallest twelve-year-old in his year.

"Back again Jeremy?" the old, skinny woman at the ticket booth croaked.

"I'm not here to cause trouble, I promise." Jeremy winked at her as he took out his wallet. "Damn, I haven't got any cash." Liam looked over to see his brother's empty leather wallet and took out his own.

"I've got this one," he said, handing over his pocket money and taking their tickets. As they walked into the crowded amusement park Liam looked at his brother's mischievous grin. "How often do you come here?"

"Just occasionally when I'm with my mates," Jeremy admitted slyly. "It's a decent place to pass the time."

Liam passed Jeremy his half of the game tickets and after a game or two they found themselves hungry from the lack of family dinner that evening and joined the queue at a snack booth behind a group of teenagers Liam thought he may have recognised from school. All too old for him to spend time with, though.

When the two brothers finally got through the rowdy group and to the front of the line the round woman in the booth looked exasperated. "Teenagers," she shrugged.

"What do you recommend?" Liam asked.

"They're all good," she snapped at him. Then with a gentler tone she continued. "Best handmade sweets around."

"You make them yourself?" Liam asked curiously as he took in all the different shapes and colours presented to him.

"Course I do. That's why they taste so good. Here," she said, placing a mixture of sweets into a paper bag and handing them over to him. "Mrs. Millar's finest selection."

"Fancy a ride on the roller coaster?" Jeremy asked, putting his arm around his younger brother's neck and steering him in that direction.

"Not particularly," Liam replied as he stuck a red gummy in his mouth. Jeremy shoved his hand in the striped paper bag and helped himself to several sweets, placing them all in his mouth at once.

"Come on, it'll be fun," Jeremy nagged as they joined the short line for the ride. A family of two excited kids and two tired looking parents took their place behind them.

Liam gave in. "Alright, just one go." Something didn't feel right in the pit of his stomach, as if it was telling him to turn and go the other way. Or, perhaps it was simply the sugar.

Wordlessly, the brothers stood next to each other and waited for their turn on the ride. Liam watched nervously as each cart rose higher on the structure and then suddenly slid down on the steep decline and whizzed through the loops with such speed he felt butterflies in his chest just from watching.

A quick glance at his brother told him that Jeremy didn't share any of his worries: his older brother was still searching his phone, presumably for any sign of alternate company.

With a deep sigh, Liam finally asked his brother the question that had been on his mind all evening. "You said something didn't you? To Mum and Dad. Why do you try to work them up like that?"

Jeremy looked up quickly. Was it his imagination, Liam wondered, or was there a flash of guilt in his eyes? He tucked away his phone. "Look, I didn't realise they would freak out like that."

"Yes, you did." Liam rolled his eyes as they took another step closer to the ride.

"Okay, maybe I did."

"Maybe you don't care when they're like that, but I do." Somehow, they'd reached the front of the queue.

Liam tucked what was left of his dinner into his pocket and they both took their seat in the cart. He fidgeted while he waited for the ride to begin, uncomfortable already. The seats were cushioned with leather that should have been bright but was pockmarked and faded; the bar in front of them was icy against his hands.

Once again, he felt anxiety take hold of his stomach and he searched the faces of the rest of the park goers to see if any of them seemed to feel the way he did. Was it some sort of sign trying to stop him from going on the ride? Liam wondered. He had never much believed in signs. No, he told himself. It must have just been normal anxiety about going on a ride he had never been on before. Perfectly normal.

"Let's talk about this later, alright? Just enjoy the ride," Jeremy told his brother as the cart began to move forward and they both sat back.

Slowly, the cart wheeled steadily up and up and up until they were high enough to look over the whole amusement park. Liam let his eyes travel over every light, every stall and every other visitor, taking the whole experience in before the ride suddenly jolted and their cart began to move forward, shaking on top of the creaking structure.

"Wait," Jeremy said. He turned to Liam: his face was completely bloodless, his eyes standing out like pools of dirty water "This doesn't feel right. Something's wrong!"

# Chapter 2

10 Years Later

"We need to do something more exciting than just sitting at the pub. Again," Jayne, my over excited best friend sighed as she took a long gulp of her beer. Golden, curly hair fell around her sharp face, falling – as usual – out of the position she used so much hair spray to create. With a best friend as beautiful as her, it was no wonder I found it so hard to be confident about my looks. I always felt too thin around Jayne, my hair too dark, and my face too plain.

"What's wrong with sitting at the pub?" Adam asked. His large, muddy eyes searched the table for some support.

"I'm just saying, we have officially finished sixth form. All five of us have gotten into university. We can't celebrate by doing the same thing we do nearly every day!"

"Well, what did you have in mind?" Jayne's bulky boyfriend Tommy asked her with a smirk as he wrapped his thick arm around her waist. Tommy was a large lad, at least a foot and half taller than Jayne. At the start of sixth form, the three guys – Tommy, Adam and George – had decided to start going to the gym together, hyping each other up for months until they were all the size of strapping rugby players. Personally, I preferred the Indie look – all floppy hair and skinny jeans – but what did I know? I'd been happy enough to date George for the last two years, until he broke up with me.

Jayne looked desperately towards Adam for answers. A habit she had picked up when they'd had that "thing" together before she started dating Tommy.

"Don't look at me," he said with a laugh. "It was my idea to come to the pub in the first place."

The five of us sat quietly around the marked wooden table, taking swigs of our drinks.

"I have an idea," George piped up with that mischievous grin I'd always loved. I could barely even look at him without a tough knot forming in the back of my throat.

"Yes?" Jayne sat up excitedly in her chair.

"Do you guys remember that old amusement park that closed down a while ago? It was a little way out of town by the woods." He looked around the group waiting for someone to confirm they knew what he was talking about. When nobody replied he carried on. "Well, anyway, I heard some guys from my business class talking about how they found it's remains still there. It's a twenty-minute walk out of town."

"Oh yeah, wait," Adam agreed. "I think I know the one you mean. My mum used to make my older sister take me there all the time. It's been closed for ten years, hasn't it?"

"Why?" Jayne asked.

"Didn't someone fall off one of the rides and die?" Tommy remembered. "He was our age at the time, I think." Everyone went quiet and stared at their drinks. Death was always one of those things you could feel bad about when you heard it on the news, but when it was someone in your town or even someone in the same school as you, it became a little too real.

Condensation dripped down my pint glass and onto the soggy paper coaster provided by the pub.

"So, do you guys want to walk up there and get a look at it?" George grinned pulling everyone from their thoughtful silence.

"Let's do it," Tommy said. He was always eager to prove how fearless he was.

"Yeah," Adam said, trying to keep up.

"It'll be different," Jayne said.

"Mae?" The group all looked my way with hopeful eyes. My heart sank. George knew I didn't like dark, creepy, abandoned places. I wondered if he'd only suggested it because he thought I would say no and they could go without me. But how could I say no? It was bad enough losing George, I didn't want to lose the rest of the group too.

I sighed deeply. "Why not?"

Everyone finished off their drinks and stood to leave while I drank mine more slowly. A nice warm, well-lit pub was much more my thing than exploring dark, abandoned amusement parks.

George led us first to the Co-op, "for supplies," he told us. A chill ran down my spine as we waited outside for his return, the warmth that had blanketed my bare arms earlier that evening totally gone. I tugged my new, thin, Free People jumper over my head and wrapped my arms around myself.

George returned with a crate of Budweiser and a big bag of Cool Ranch Doritos, and handed out a beer to each of us and we were back on our way again.

As we made our way down the dark pathways through the forest, I couldn't help but glance behind me at the disappearing street lights, almost like they were taking with them what little enthusiasm I had forced myself to muster for the evening. We ventured off the path and pushed our way through the thick undergrowth, dodging branches and tall tree roots. The darkness grew as we got further into the forest. The glow from the street lights behind us was replaced with the shadow of leaves and tree trunks.

I stumbled slightly as I lifted my boots over a particularly high and thick mossy tree root. Adam stuck his hands out from where he was walking behind me and held onto my waist to steady me. I thanked him awkwardly, feeling the warmth from his fingers seep through to the skin beneath my thin skater dress. He let go with a nod and looked down at his feet as we continued. His skin was so dark, I thought I might lose him in the forest if it wasn't for his bright choice in clothing.

Jayne giggled from ahead where she was holding excitedly onto Tommy's hand. Jayne was always up for an adventure or a spooky exploration, perhaps that was why her relationship was still going strong and mine wasn't. I stared at their entwined fingers as they walked, before noticing

George's hand hanging beside him, almost inviting me to take hold of it. I could still feel the touch of his hand around mine, how comfortable it had been, even if it was all in my head now.

"Do you actually know where you're going?" I called to George, irritated by the lingering feelings I had for him. It had been two months already so why couldn't I get over him?

He hesitated before answering, glancing quickly over his shoulder. "I'm sure it's just up here." As he said it I noticed that in front of us the tree branches were beginning to separate, allowing the small beams of moonlight to peek through. Everyone else must have noticed the clearing ahead too, because we all suddenly sped up.

I wanted nothing more than to turn around and go home, but the thought of wandering through the spooky forest by myself was enough to convince me to stay with the group.

"Here it is!" George called back to us all, as he stepped out of the dark forest.

The moon cast an eerie silver glow on the rusty remains of the old amusement park. There wasn't much left to look at, just a few old structures that may have been some sort of roller coasters, smaller frames that looked like they were there to support the rides, but the rides themselves were gone.

Adam remembered only small details from the few times he had come to this amusement park with his older sister, but I had no memory of it from before that night; my parents had never been interested in that type of thing.

The group stepped over a patch of broken glass that must have been left by the last lot of teenagers looking for something memorable to do with their evening. No-one spoke as we ventured through the grounds that must have once been filled with lights and liveliness.

"Well, this is a bit of let down," Adam scoffed. "There's barely anything left. Basically, just a load of rusty metal."

"Alright, alright," George said, his face filled with disappointment. "I heard some guys in my business class talking about it. It sounded much cooler from what they said."

"Should we just go back then?" I asked, as casually as I could make it.

"No," Jayne said, forever the optimist. "Let's just sit a while. That's all we were going to do at the pub, may as well do it here."

Looking around for a comfy spot we finally found somewhere that looked safe enough. Although as soon as we were sitting a menacing shadow seemed to seep from the surrounding forest, getting closer the more I looked at it and an odd feeling itched at my back, almost like someone was watching us. The half-moon created just enough light to see each other in our little circle seated around the box of beer.

"Who would have thought, that first day in year twelve, we'd be here together a couple of years later?" Adam said.

We all grinned at each other.

The five of us had become friends quickly when we had all joined the same sixth form; just a random mix of people who didn't know anyone else, apart from me and George. On the first day I was sitting on my own at the back of the common room on one of the old, tatty chairs provided only for sixth-formers. Jayne had walked into the room with her head down and went straight for the seat next to me, looking up only when she had safely settled herself into her chair.

I smiled at her politely thinking she looked like she might be too shy to make friends herself. Little did I know that she would soon become the loudest member of our group. She told me that she liked my floral shirt, which I had bought especially for the first day of sixth form, and after that it seemed like we could never run out of things to talk about.

George had made his way over to where Jayne and I were now discussing our chosen classes with a guy next to him that I soon found out was Adam. They had just met when they discovered their lockers were right next to each other and apparently bonded instantly when George spotted a Fortnite sticker on Adam's notebook.

Two minutes into the head of sixth form's speech, a boy rushed into the room, clattering the zips of his bag on the doors and causing the speech to come to a stop and the whole room to stare his way.

"Sorry!" he called as he located the only free seat in the room which happened to be on our row next to Jayne. When the speech finally came to an end, he introduced himself as Tommy, winked at Jayne, and somehow that was all it took for us to become friends.

From that day forward we all met in the sixth form common room during breaks and free periods and it wasn't long before we were all meeting up after school and on weekends.

"But here we are," Jayne said. "Reminiscing on the best years of our lives in the middle of a derelict amusement park."

"I hardly think these are the best years of our lives," Adam scoffed at Jayne's comment. He swung his legs out in front of him leaning back on his arms.

"It all gets very serious at university though, doesn't it?" She said.

"I thought university was supposed to be the best years of your life," I said. It was something I had been asking myself for a while now. "You know, new places, new experiences, new people."

"Bit harsh, Mae," George snapped at the last bit. I didn't meet his eyes, or anyone else's, but I could tell that my comment hadn't gone down well with any of them.

"I don't want new people though, I like these people," Jayne huffed as she wriggled further into her boyfriend's broad chest. I tried desperately to ignore the pain shooting through my own seeing the two of them getting close to each other, enjoying each other's touch, when out the corner of my eye I could see George sipping at his beer, his body still as inviting to me as it always had been.

"This is getting a bit depressing for me, let's talk about something else," Tommy suggested.

"Let's play truth or dare!" Jayne exclaimed, just as excited as usual. "Mae, you first. Truth or dare?"

I took in a deep breath. "I'll just watch while you guys play."

"Come on Mae, just play one round. You've gotten so boring since George broke up with you." Tension filled the air between us just as quickly as the words fell from her mouth. Jaynes dark eyes grew wide as she realised what she'd said.

I stared at her. Maybe I had gotten a bit boring, but how could I not? My heart had been broken. I'd continued putting the effort in with this group when soon we would all be living in different parts of the country and would likely no longer be talking. And now Jayne had turned on me. And she'd done it in front of George.

"Oh right, so you genuinely think you and Tommy will still be dating this time next year? Even though you'll be living on opposite sides of the country," I snapped back.

"Of course, we will," she said defensively, taking Tommy's hand tightly in hers. "We're going to make long distance work. Right?"

Her hopeful, stubborn eyes turned sharply to Tommy's. Taken aback by being put in the middle of an argument that clearly wasn't meant for him, Tommy flushed red.

"I mean," he began, "hopefully."

Jayne gasped, sitting up straight to face him fully. "What the hell?"

Tommy swallowed nervously. "Well, it's just that a lot of couples don't do well with long distance."

Jayne stared at him as if expecting him to go on.

"I just don't want you getting set on the hope that we'll be together forever when statistically couples our age don't last during a long-distance relationship."

"So, you want to break up?" Jayne's voice was shrill and she folded her arms defiantly across her chest.

"Not right now," Tommy replied desperately. Poor guy, I thought to myself. How had I put him in this position?

"But you want to break up at some point."

"That's not what – "

"Guys, wait," George shushed them, sitting up from where he had been silently observing the conflict. "What's that?"

All at once our eyes followed his finger to where lights were flashing through the tree branches, approaching with speed.

"Someone's coming!" I whispered frantically, getting to my feet. We all froze, unsure where to run as the lights were coming from the only path we knew.

"Who's there?" shouted a loud voice from the trees. "This is private property!"

Tommy grabbed Jayne's hand and mouthed "hide" to everyone else. I looked around at the broken pieces of rides for somewhere to hide. Spotting a square shaped wall with bricks missing by the edge of the forest, I ran to it and dived, crouching low to the ground. There were old bricks fallen and scattered around the outside. I leant my back against the wall and tried to steady my breathing.

I hadn't seen where any of the others had gone but I hoped they would locate me before vacating the area, the thought of sneaking around this place by myself in the dark made my anxious heart beat even faster than it already was.

Fallen leaves crunched under the footsteps of the approaching officer. His torch flashed in my direction a few times, and I held my breath as I imagined the trouble I was about to get into.

Just as I expected the face of an angry officer to peer around the wall at my hiding spot the crunching grew quieter and he retreated back the way he had come. I lifted myself off the ground and peeked my head over the wall to try and spot any of the others from my group. I must've kicked a stone as something cracked, alerting the officer to look my way again.

I ducked down and turned my back to the wall once again. Only this time when I turned around, I noticed the sudden appearance of a pair of glowing sapphire eyes. The colour was so brilliant and deep I couldn't bring myself to look away, in fact I felt myself leaning forward into them.

His hand reached out for mine and I took it without hesitation. At first my skin felt almost numb against his, but as he led me into the deep forest behind him the feeling returned to my fingers and soon I felt his thumb rubbing my palm.

I didn't look back as we made our way further and further into the forest, all I could focus on was his eyes.

# Chapter 3

It felt like a dream. Everything was blurry around the edges and I could only see what I set my mind on. I didn't see where we went or which turns we took. I was led only by my desire to watch the boy leading me.

How long had we been walking for? Or were we drifting?

I focused my attention away from his ocean eyes and took in his other features. His hair was brown and shaggy like it hadn't been cut for a while, his nose was slim and pointed just a little on the end. With the rest of his skin so pale his rosy cheeks stood out in the dark. Maybe it was the moonlight that brought out his cheekbones. His fitted shirt suggested a fit body underneath, but not one that was bulky from hours a day at the gym like my friends, but muscular as if he were a sportsman. I bit my lip. Did my face look smooth and blush in the moonlight? I wondered to myself. Was my short hair just a mess of muddy colours or had it somehow managed to survive the night's torments with a somewhat neat fringe and tidy sides tucked behind my ears.

"Where are we going?" I asked.

"You'll see." His voice sounded in my mind as if he hadn't said anything at all. If I hadn't seen his plump lips move, I would have thought I'd imagined his reply.

The eagerness in his voice and eyes were almost childlike. Even still, there was an uneasy feeling behind my attraction to him. Was I being taken? What did he want with me?

The boy was pulling me faster through the now glowing forest. Emerald leaves and bronze branches parted for us, creating a beautiful pathway through the nature he was sharing with me.

He stopped abruptly, turning his back to me slowly.

"Are you ready?" he asked me.

"Yes." How could I say no?

A grin as beautiful as crystals spread once again across his face as he pulled branches to the side and waited patiently for me to step through to the dazzling lights awaiting me.

Glowing colours surprised my vision like opening your bedroom curtains first thing on a clear summer morning. Squinting, I made my way cautiously forward.

First, I noticed a tall structure in the distance with a cart travelling with speed through the loops and curves. Joyous screams filled my ears.

Below the working ride were booths of games and challenges, queues of people trailed from each one waiting their turn to contribute to the night's enjoyment. Colourful workers were spread throughout, encouraging their guests to participate in every exciting activity.

In front of me was a tall arch providing entrance into the wonderful world beyond. Bright white lights filled the arch spelling out "Jeremy's Amusement Park".

I couldn't believe my awestruck eyes. Where had it come from? It was so bright I couldn't understand how I hadn't seen it in the distance. How had I made it almost to its front door before noticing it was there?

The boy's hand remained tightly around mine as he pulled me forward under the archway and into the midst of magical chaos.

My eyes searched the crowds for a sign or an answer to the curiosity swimming through me. I spotted a couple laughing at the booth closest to us. The man, tall and skinny in a smart shirt, threw tennis balls at the pins stacked a few feet in front of him. The woman, with a slim figure and glossy blonde hair that bounced as she did, jumped up and down as her partner knocked over pins and won her a fluffy teddy bear.

A plump family of four made their way to the front of the line for the roller coaster and climbed into the bright cart. The two teenagers sat in front of their parents who were sitting with their arms tightly together. The mother's thin eyebrows were scrunched together with nerves I could see even from a distance away.

A man in a white shirt and a glossy auburn waistcoat wrapped his hand tightly around the lever. His curly grey mustache lifted as he grinned at the excited kids aboard. He pulled the lever quickly and the cart was on its way, rising higher and higher on the sturdy structure.

A group of teenage boys crowded around a candy floss stand with pink and white stripes covering its walls.

"Two tickets?" A gruff woman's voice interrupted my thoughts and brought my attention away from the other guests. I hadn't seen the stand as we walked in but we were now standing right next to a small table with a glittery table cloth, a padlocked box with a hole for money deposits, and a ticket dispenser.

The boy took the tickets and thanked her cheerily before taking me further into the throng of excitement. I hadn't seen him pay.

"Well?" he said looking hopefully down into my eyes. Unsure what the question was referring to I couldn't answer his expectant question. "Is it everything you were hoping for?"

"What do you mean?"

"The park." His grin was quickly growing on me, and I could hardly stop my own mouth from doing the same. "Isn't it amazing?"

"It's beautiful," I agreed. "Has this always been here?"

"Only for a few years." He looked away for the first time since I'd met him. "What shall we do first?"

I looked around us, overwhelmed by the amount of choice we had. Would I like rides or games?

"You choose," I told him.

He pulled me over to a game close by. I was handed three darts and told to aim at the water balloons pinned to the wall behind the counter. He had his own set in his hand but waited patiently for me to go first. I had never been particularly good at darts.

I lifted one of the darts up to eye level and tested it out a couple of times moving it back and forth. I threw it with what felt like perfect aim, releasing the dart with a straight arm. Somehow, I missed all the balloons and my dart landed against the wall in between a patch of stretched yellow balloons.

"That's okay," he said enthusiastically. "Try again."

I swallowed deeply and lifted another dart readying it for flight. I squinted one eye to focus on exactly where I wanted the dart to land. Releasing the dart, I watched it fly through the air and land in a blue balloon. Unfortunately, it landed just below the pin and the balloon didn't pop. I hadn't played this game before but I was fairly certain that was the aim.

"You do one," I begged him not wanting to embarrass myself further. He agreed and held his dart up with expert precision and released it with a swing of his arm. The balloon burst and water fell to the ground.

"Do another one so I can watch how you did it," I told him as I focused my eyes on his throwing arm. I watched as his biceps tightened and then released. Distracted, I missed the balloon popping. I only knew it had from the noise of the splash and the cheer from the man waiting patiently behind the counter.

Nervously, I lifted my last dart and tried to imitate his movements. Once again, I missed the balloons and the dart deflected off the wall and fell pathetically onto the ground. I avoided looking at him as I felt my embarrassment warm my cheeks.

"Here, you can have my last one," he said, passing me the dart. "Let me show you." He stepped closer to me and put his hand gently around mine. I turned to get a better look at his features and noticed a light stubble that I hadn't seen before. He was a little shorter than George, I noticed. The warmth of his hand disappeared as he released mine and the dart flew forward, landing square in the middle of a particularly large balloon, splashing water over all those surrounding it.

His body stayed close to mine as he accepted his prize. He passed me the stuffed purple teddy bear proudly. "That last one was all you, you deserve the prize."

I took it from him and looked at its light button eyes. He was a gentleman, I thought to myself. He took my hand in his again and guided me in the direction of another booth.

"Wait," I said, stopping him in his tracks. A sudden important question had just filled my mind and I had to know the answer before we went any further. "What's your name?"

"Jeremy."

"Like the name of the park?" I asked with wide eyes. He nodded in answer. "Is it yours?"

"Something like that," Jeremy laughed as we continued to the next booth.

# Chapter 4

"Well, don't you want to know my name?" I asked. Surely this man who had chosen me to show around his amusement park would want to know my name.

"Of course, I do," he said seriously. "But only if you want to tell me."

I hesitated for a moment. Why wouldn't I want to tell him? I imagined him saying my name with his musical voice and decided I needed to hear him say it. "It's Mae."

"Mae," he repeated. "Beautiful."

We stood together while people passed us, dodging our unmoving bodies as they made their way to join games with their friends. It was easy to forget there were other people there when Jeremy's dazzling eyes were on mine.

Jeremy replaced his hand in mine and turned back to join the movement around us. We arrived at a booth selling sweets and treats. Bags of radiant hard candies, displays of gummy choices and a selection of sugary shapes were all spread across the stand.

A large woman was positioned behind the counter, wearing a baby pink shirt with swirls of gold over it. Silver strands swam through her bushy scarlet curls. Her lips matched the colour of her hair, as did her teeth which were covered in smudges of her lip stick. Her eyes lit up when she spotted Jeremy coming her way. Her sight followed his arm until she spotted his hand in mine. Did her smile fade a little when she saw me?

"Hello, Lovely," she greeted him without looking my way. "What'll it be today?" He greeted her back and then introduced us.

"First time here?" Mrs. Millar asked me. I nodded, feeling intimidated not only by her size but by the way she looked at me. A smile stayed over her face but her dark eyes seemed to have a different opinion. "I have the best treat selection you will find in any park."

"She's not wrong," Jeremy assured me. "I've never tasted anything better."

Jeremy chose a small selection of sweets and Mrs. Millar placed them in a paper bag which she passed over the counter to him. "Enjoy your night," she said in a syrupy voice.

"I know somewhere nice we can sit and eat these," Jeremy announced and I followed him, just glad to be getting away from the oddly unwelcoming stare from Mrs. Millar. We wandered through a street of game booths calling out to us to play them, lights flashing as we stepped into their view. He led me away from the games and away from the flashier rides, and to the Ferris wheel.

"This is more my speed," I said, grinning, as we climbed onto our seat.

As the Ferris wheel came to a stop and we were dangling safely at the top I felt like I could finally rest from all the lights and noises. I had forgotten that this hidden wonderland was surrounded by a thick, dark forest, but from this height I could see the forest for miles. There were no other lights for a long way and I wondered how far we had really walked to get there.

I allowed my eyes to wander above the surprisingly unmenacing forest and noticed the clear sky, filled with the stars that flickered through the darkness surrounding us. Mystified by their beauty, I couldn't bring myself to look away from the amazing sight.

Jeremy placed something in my hand and I finally looked down to discover a hard sweet that matched the sight I had just been staring at; a deep cerulean shell with specks of gold throughout. "Try it," Jeremy encouraged me.

Slowly, I lifted it into my mouth. Sparks of sweetness hit my tongue instantly, a delicious warmth spread over my tastebuds and a mixture of raspberry and dark chocolate filled my senses. I eagerly took another sweet from the bag and a new taste filled my mouth; this time a sugary but fresh apple.

"They're delicious!" I told Jeremy who had been watching me.

"I knew you would like them," he announced taking one for himself.

"How did you know?"

"I could tell." Somehow that answer felt right, as if in the short amount of time we'd spent together he could have already gotten to know my tastes.

We sat together in a delicious silence until all the sweets were gone. Curiously the noise from the park didn't reach us at that height. It felt as though we had found the only private spot in the whole park. Below us, the people were so small they almost looked like toys rather than living beings.

Jeremy's knee knocked against mine as the light breeze rocked our little cart. The air was so fresh and undisturbed at the top of the Ferris wheel that it felt silky smooth as I sucked it into my lungs. My mind felt clearer up there and thoughts and questions began to fill me up.

"Why did you bring me here?" I asked Jeremy curiously, remembering for the first time since arriving there that I was supposed to be with my friends.

"It's a nice place for having a snack."

"No, I mean why did you bring me to your park. Why did you choose me?"

Jeremy took a deep breath and lowered his eyes to his hands folded in his lap. "You looked so disappointed when you saw that old broken-down park earlier, so I thought this might cheer you up."

"You were watching us?" Oddly I didn't feel scared by this fact. Rather, a small part of me felt embarrassed that he might have seen the way I had kept looking at George when I thought he wouldn't notice or the things I had said to Jayne.

"Only you," he admitted shyly. "Not the others."

"But why me?"

He lifted his face to mine and once again I was captivated by his eyes so close to mine. "I don't know. There's just something about you."

What could he possibly have seen in me? In the dark glow of the moon and the shadows of the surrounding trees, I sat with my friends refusing to participate in their games, and somehow that had caused him to notice me.

A chill ran down the back of my bare neck and I tried to hide my shiver. My attempt to stop Jeremy from noticing didn't work and he gently rested his arm around my shoulders, the warmth of his body radiated into my own and I let myself relax against him.

It was the first time in a while that I'd had a boy's attention like this, and I suddenly realised how long we had been motionless at the top of the Ferris wheel.

"Why hasn't the ride moved for so long?"

"I asked them to give us a little time together," Jeremy smirked. "I'll signal at the attendant when we're ready to come down."

It must be one of the perks of owning your own amusement park, I thought.

"What's your favourite part about the park?" I asked him as we both watched the events happening around us.

"I just love seeing how happy it makes people." I could hear the smile on his face as he talked without having to turn around and see the dimples forming on his cheeks. "I used to go to an amusement park with my friends all the time. I even brought my younger brother once."

"Has he been here?" I asked, imagining a second Jeremy with a younger face.

"No," The smile faded from his face. "I haven't seen him for a while."

"Why not?" I asked before I could stop myself.

His smile disappeared completely. "It's…
Complicated."

"I'm sorry, I shouldn't have asked." I felt
like a complete failure. He had brought me there to
make me happy and all I was doing was ruining his
good mood. I thought quickly of something I could
say to bring back the sparkle in his eyes. "I haven't
been to an amusement park in so long, I had
forgotten how fun they are. I'd love to see some
more of it."

"You would?" he asked excitedly. "Well,
let's go." With that he waved to someone below us
and the Ferris wheel began to move again and we
left behind our peaceful haven and rejoined the
colourful world below.

Jeremy took me to some more game booths
and we laughed at my failed attempts to play at the
same practiced standards as him. It was clear he had
played each of the games many, many times before.

I carried my stuffed animal that Jeremy had
won stifling a yawn as we made our way to the next
game.

"You're tired?" He seemed confused by the
notion.

"Well, I have been here all night," I
reasoned with him, suddenly noticing the change of
colour in the sky. I felt panic catch at my heart – my
friends would be frantic. I couldn't understand how
it had happened. The evening had seemed to pass
us by in a blur.

"All night?" His eyes lifted to the
lightening sky. "But there's so much left to see."

He seemed so disappointed, I told myself I should stay a little longer. I'd been there that long, what's a little longer?

"Why don't we have a go on the roller coaster, I'm sure that'll wake me up," I suggested.

Horror spread across Jeremy's face so suddenly it took my breath away. "No, we can't. It's not safe."

I gasped looking at all the people currently riding it. "How do you know? We need to tell someone if it's not safe."

Before Jeremy could reply Mrs. Millar appeared behind us. "I think it's time your friend made her way home," she said sternly, shuffling us in the direction of the exit.

Jeremy looked as though he may fight the issue but changed his mind. "You're right." He walked me to the entry of the park and showed me the path to follow to get back to the abandoned amusement park where I had first seen him. "You'll come back tomorrow though, right?"

"Of course, I will," I agreed without hesitation, watching Jeremy's eyebrows relax. "How will I find my way back?"

"You'll find it, I know you will." He grinned at me again for the last time that evening, before turning me towards the exit. "I'll meet you here at midnight."

# Chapter 5

I didn't remember walking back or how long it had taken me; I couldn't even picture the route I'd taken. But somehow, I stepped through the trees and found myself standing in the abandoned amusement park. In the light of day, it looked even smaller than it had the evening before, full of rusted iron structures and weeds overtaking what would have been the paths.

A vibrating noise caught my attention and I discovered my phone behind the wall I had been hiding behind. It must have fallen out when I'd crouched down in order to not be seen by the officer.

I answered the call not looking at who was calling.

"Mae!" gasped Jayne from the other end of the call. "Where have you been? We've been looking for you all night."

"I..." Where had I been? As I looked around me more of the night's events were becoming fuzzy. "I met this guy last night."

"You met a guy?" Jayne sounded offended. "Is that where you've been? You could have let us know; we've been searching the woods all night. I almost called the police!"

I stepped over the forgotten machinery and reentered the forest on the opposite side of the grounds. At least I could remember the way we had gotten to the abandoned park in the first place.

"I'm sorry," I replied pathetically.

Jayne sighed into the phone. "Who was it then?"

"Who was what?" I asked deliriously.

"Who was the guy you met last night?" She tutted as if it was a silly question.

"Oh, his name was..." What was his name? I racked my brain, sure he had told me at some point. "I... I can't remember."

"You can't remember?" Jayne laughed. "How much did you drink?"

I'd almost forgotten we'd been drinking at all.

"Look, Jayne, is it alright if I give you a call later? I'm feeling a little fuzzy this morning." I hung up and made my way home. It was still early and with any luck I'd be able to sneak in the house without my parents noticing and pretend like I had been there all night.

I snuck through the back door and closed it gently behind me. The modern house was beautifully lit with the shining sun diving through the large windows. When my parents had bought the house it had been newly built, and over the years they had updated small parts, but mostly it stayed the same as when we moved in.

"Mae?" That was my mum's quizzical voice. I turned to see her standing next to the kettle while it boiled. "Were you out all night?"

"I stayed at Jayne's," I lied quickly. It was something I did so often I could be sure she'd believe me.

"You should have told me if you weren't coming home," she sighed, lifting an eyebrow in that unimpressed way of hers.

"Sorry mum, I'll send you a text next time."

"I left the doors unlocked for you," she told me. "Anyone could've gotten in."

"I'll take my key next time."

She took a second cup out of the cupboard and poured a scoop of instant coffee into it. I could tell she had more she wanted to say. In order to get back into her good graces I fetched the milk from the fridge and poured a drop into both cups when they had been filled with boiling water. My mum passed me one of the cups and we sat together at the square kitchen table.

"I know you're an adult now, Mae," she started. That was the same way she started every lecture she'd given me since my eighteenth birthday. "But you still live in my house, and you need to respect that."

"You're right, Mum, I'm sorry." I admitted my defeat and left her to enjoy her coffee in peace, taking mine to my room.

I sat on my neatly made bed and tried desperately to remember the events of the night before. I remembered the five of us going to the abandoned amusement park. Things started to get blurry when the officer showed up and we all dispersed in different directions.

I had met someone. But who? It felt like I had dreamt the whole thing and I'd woken up only to forget the details. Was it possible that it was a dream? Had I drunk more than I remembered and passed out behind that old wall?

I peeled off the outfit I had been wearing for almost twenty-four hours and climbed into the refreshing shower, feeling the heat swim down my body, thinking that a shower and a clean set of clothes might clear my mind enough to make the blurry images of the light and the crowds and him come into focus. But as I pulled my shirt over my head, I realised the memories were not coming back.

The doorbell rang before I had a chance to dry my dripping hair. Jayne stood at the front door with an irritated expression pasted over her face.

"So, you're fine then?" she asked as she stormed through the door and straight into the kitchen. "I've been up all night thinking we had gotten you abducted and then this morning I found out you were just getting it on with some guy you met. Where would you have even met him? In the woods?"

I closed the door and followed her into the kitchen where she was pouring herself a glass of orange juice. She offered me a glass through a hand gesture and I declined. We sat at the table before I opened up to her.

"To be honest, Jayne, I really can't remember much about last night."

She rolled her eyes before realising the seriousness of the situation. "Wait, did your drink get spiked?"

"I don't know how it could, I was with you guys all night before that," I confessed.

"What about that guy you met? Do you think he could have done it?"

"I didn't even have a drink when I was with him," I told her, although I wasn't sure if that was the truth or not. "Besides, I'm starting to think maybe I imagined him."

"What are you going to do then?" she asked.

"What do you mean?"

"Should we report this to the police? I mean, you may have been drugged and you barely remember any of the night. That's a bit concerning."

Panic took hold of my chest. "We can't call the police!" I snapped. Although I couldn't remember much, I didn't feel as though anything had happened to warrant that kind of response. Besides, what if it had all been a drunken dream? I could have imagined the whole thing.

"Why not? This sounds serious."

"No, Jayne. Don't tell anyone about this, okay?"

Jayne sighed in defeat. "Well, if he is real are you going to see him again?" As she said it the memory of the boy telling me to return at midnight floated into my consciousness. I couldn't tell if it was real but I had to go back to see if it was all a part of my wild, drunk imagination. I decided not to share this possible memory with Jayne.

"Tommy and I are fine by the way," she informed me. "No thanks to you."

For now, I thought to myself bitterly.

Even though I had never admitted it I had always believed that my relationship with George had been stronger than Jayne and Tommy's. I thought that we had more in common than they did, that we would last longer. It wasn't meant to be a competition but with Jayne constantly all over Tommy sometimes it felt like she was trying to show off her perfect relationship.

The image of the mysterious boy's sapphire eyes flashed through my mind, and a warm feeling swam through my chest. Perhaps, it was him I was supposed to be with all along. I decided I didn't want to share him with Jayne. She had her relationship, and he could be mine.

# Chapter 6

I sat by myself at the kitchen table for a long time after Jayne left. All kinds of questions were flying through my mind. One question stood out from the rest. Was it real?

I had to know.

The decision was made; I would go back that night and find out once and for all if this boy was real, and what had really happened the night before. The plan was pretty straight-forward, I would sneak out the house at eleven pm giving myself an hour to find it again, starting with locating the abandoned amusement park.

I ate dinner with my parents that evening and then went to my room to get some sleep before another evening without.

After only two hours of sleep, I pulled myself out of my warm, tempting bed and got dressed. I decided to wear something a little warmer that night, with tight jeans, a suede jacket and comfortable trainers.

I couldn't stop myself from taking the time to apply some simple make up, just in case I saw him again. I couldn't deny that I was hoping I would. There was something intriguing about him, I just couldn't figure out what. The only clear memory of the night before was the way he had made me feel.

I knew I should be worried about the fact I couldn't remember any of the night before, but for some reason I felt very calm. Almost too calm. That felt more concerning to me than losing my memory in the first place.

The house was quiet as I crept out my bedroom that evening. Mum had a double shift at the local café/restaurant she managed and wouldn't be home until late and dad appeared to be in bed already. Making my way through the dark house I hoped desperately that tonight's expedition would lead to some answers.

Locking the door behind myself I made my way quickly out of town and towards the woodland path.

"Mae?" George's voice came from behind me. I froze, straightening my spine as my mind raced with all the excuses I could think of for why I was there.

I turned round. "Hey," I said naturally. "What are you doing out here?"

"I'm just on my way home from Adam's," he said casually, nodding his head the way he was walking, as if I didn't know where he lived. Until we broke up a few months before I had been at George's house most afternoons.

"Oh yeah?" I played it cool and tried to keep the conversation off of myself. "Fortnight?"

He shrugged. "Nah, some other game he just downloaded."

I nodded. George and I hadn't been together, just the two of us, since the breakup and I didn't know exactly how to act. All I wanted to do was run in the opposite direction.

"Mae – " George began.

"Well, I better get on," I interrupted, taking a few steps back. "See ya."

George opened his mouth as though he might say something else, but in the end he left it. "See ya."

I hurried quickly along the path before George could change his mind and say whatever it was he was thinking about. He must have been wondering where I was the night before; they all knew I had disappeared without a word. I wondered if Jayne had told them all that I'd said I'd met someone.

Once again, I found my way into the forest away from the main path, away from the friendly street lights and into the shadowy darkness. I looked over my shoulder constantly, nervous to see the light slowly evaporating behind the thick layers of leaves.

There was no real path to follow here and I just hoped I was going the right way. I had no indication of which route was the right one. It didn't feel like we had made many turns when George led us the night before so I decided the safest bet was to go straight.

Had it taken this long last night? I wondered to myself nervously, my heart beating in my ears. Darkness surrounded my ankles and I realised I couldn't see my feet. I began walking a lot more carefully to avoid tripping on low hanging branches and roots I couldn't see.

Finally, I saw a clearing ahead, lit up by the bright moon in the clear sky. I felt my feet speeding up as I was suddenly overtaken by a desperation to get out of the woods.

There it was: the old, rusty amusement park, covered in dead leaves. Scanning it quickly I ensured there were no other young people exploring it that I might run into. Deciding the coast was clear I took a step forward and examined the structures.

A vision flashed before my eyes and I saw myself walking back into the forest, I saw a blurry hand covering mine, and his eyes. I had to figure out where to reenter the forest. Would he be waiting for me, to lead me once again to... Where did he take me?

Remembering the officer's torches approaching us I was able to find my way back to the wall I had hidden behind. As I stepped behind the fallen wall and turned to the forest beyond, I noticed something small and furry. Soft against the palm of my hand, I held it, inspecting the light eyes of the teddy bear.

He had won it for me, I remembered suddenly. But how? It had to be a sign that this was the way I should be going.

With a deep breath I stepped back into the forest. As I did the unbelievable events of the night before came flooding back to me. Jeremy, his amusement park, Mrs. Millar, the Ferris wheel and the sweets. It was like the sun flashing in my eyes leaving behind a blind spot, only the blind spot was filled with memories and feelings I only just remembered having.

# Chapter 7

The flashing of memories turned quickly into the flashing of lights and screams of enjoyment. How was it possible? I'd taken one step into the forest and already I was stepping out at the other side and into the fantastic amusement park.

"Two nights in a row?" the woman at the ticket table asked with a bored tone in her voice.

I didn't have time to answer before I spotted Jeremy only a few feet away, quickly jumping towards me. He wrapped his arms around my waist and lifted me off the ground in an unexpected bear hug full of warmth and a spicy scent. "You came!" he exclaimed.

"How could I not?" I laughed as he released me back onto my unsteady legs.

"I was worried I wouldn't see you again," Jeremy confessed, with his large ocean eyes looking down shyly. He was in the same pair of loose jeans and fitted shirt that he had worn the night before. It looked great on him, but I wondered why he hadn't changed. I hoped he appreciated the new outfit I'd chosen for that night.

"What shall we do tonight then?" I ask with a grin. I was ecstatic to find out he was real and to remember the fun we'd had the night before. I didn't question why I had forgotten it all or why the memories had all come back when I returned, I was just happy to be back at Jeremy's Amusement Park.

Jeremy's grin matched mine as he took my hand in his and led me through the thriving amusement park to a teepee shaped tent, covered in ruby tassels and fairy lights all around it. Long, heavy curtains were pinned open as if inviting us in.

Hushed candle lights awaited us inside, on top of a round table covered in a thin paisley cloth. "Join me," the woman said softly from where she sat, cross legged, behind the table. Jeremy closed the curtain door and we settled ourselves on the cushions provided on the opposite side. The fortune teller had a golden scarf holding down her wiry black hair and thick jewelry around her neck. Thick black shadow lined her eyes and her crooked teeth stood out even in the gloom.

"Have you come to find out your fortune?" she croaked.

I glanced in Jeremy's direction and he nodded his encouragement. "Yes," I replied nervously. I had never particularly liked the idea of fortune tellers or knowing anything about the future. I preferred not to worry myself with things that could so easily go the wrong way.

"Look here," she said, lifting her hands onto the table and resting them around a crystal ball. Her hands moved slowly in a circular motion around the sphere and a smoky red glow began to appear inside. "What would you like to know?"

My mind went blank and I tried to think of a good question to ask. Would I enjoy university? Would I get a good job? Would I find love? The last one hung on the end of my tongue as I felt the presence of Jeremy beside me. His encouraging smile and enchanting eyes were hard to resist, but did he feel the same about me?

"I see something," the fortune teller began before I could actually voice one of my many questions. "So, it is love you have questions about?"

I hoped the blush heating my cheeks would be disguised by the glow of the ball in front of me. I kept my eyes straight ahead of me and tried to forget that Jeremy could hear everything being said.

"You will find love," she hummed with her eyes closed, rocking gently where she sat. Suddenly she gasped and the glow turned dark as blood. "Yes, you will find love, but it is not who or when you expect."

I could feel my eyebrows drawing tighter together. Was that the kind of non-specific prediction that was supposed to make me beg for more answers? It wouldn't work.

"What about Jeremy?" I asked trying to take the attention away from myself and curious as to what she had to say about his love life.

The red mist drained instantly from the ball, leaving it only with its bare crystal remains. "No," she said stubbornly. "I cannot tell the fortune of someone with no future."

"What's that supposed to mean?" I demanded.

"That's all I have for you today," the fortune teller told us plainly, sitting back on her silk cushion and closing her eyes.

"But –" I began furiously.

"Let's go," Jeremy said quietly. The smile was still on his face, but he looked disappointed. He helped me to my feet and then held the curtains open for me to walk through. He didn't pin them open again as they had been when we arrived, instead he let the curtain fall back into place, closing the tent off from the rest of the park. A shadow seemed to have fallen over the mysterious tent and a chill ran through me as we walked back into the lights of the park.

"Why don't we give the roller coaster a go?" I suggested trying to bring his spirits back up.

"We can't," he muttered without looking my way.

"Come on, I think it'll be fun." I nudged his arm playfully but he pulled it away quickly.

"I told you last night, it isn't safe," he snapped.

"But all those people are riding it now…" I trailed off as I noticed a familiar couple in the queue for the roller coaster. The slim couple with beautiful hair that I had seen the night before were back for the second night in a row. She hung off his arm with excitement just as she had when I had seen them the night before playing one of the games. Was she in the same pretty dress she'd worn the day before?

"Let's get something to eat," Jeremy suggested, leading me away. I found myself standing in front of the sweets stall again. Mrs. Millar was staring down at me with one eyebrow raised and a purse in her lips.

"Back again?" she questioned me.

"Yes," I challenged her. I got the feeling she wasn't happy with my being there and I couldn't put my finger on why. I wondered how close Jeremy really was to her. Could Mrs. Millar be a family friend? If she was, shouldn't she want Jeremy to make friends?

Jeremy ignored the tension between us and ordered two bags of colourful candy floss. He passed one to me and led me away.

"Goodbye," Mrs. Millar called mysteriously to our backs. I glanced over my shoulder to see her dark eyes glued to our retreating figures.

# Chapter 8

A plump family of four passed us as we wandered away from the sweet stall. I felt a shock of blood rush through my body as I recognised them from the night before too. In fact, the more I looked around I realised I recognised all the faces around me. They had all been there the night before. They were all dressed in the same clothes they had been wearing the night before.

"Were all these people here before?" I asked Jeremy, wondering if he had even noticed.

"Of course, they are always here." He said it so matter-of-factly I almost didn't question him further.

"But, why?" Jeremy's quizzical stare told me he didn't see why it would be strange. "Why do the same people always come back?"

"They were all here when it happened."

I didn't understand what he meant or if he thought there was something I should have already known. "What do you mean? What happened?"

Jeremy stopped walking and turned to me. He was about half a foot taller than me, looking down into my curious eyes. His light stubble hadn't grown at all in a day and his hair remained long and uncut. As usual the glorious blue of his eyes enchanted me, and left me tongue-tied and confused.

The corners of his plump lips turned up as he watched me. "Why don't we play another game?" he said gently. Part of me knew he was avoiding answering my queries but I couldn't resist his beautiful face. He raised his hand and tucked my short fridge to the side of my face.

"Why did you invite me back tonight?" I asked him curiously as I held his eye contact and cherished the feel of his fingers in my hair.

"I like your company," he admitted. "You make me laugh. And we had a good time together last night, didn't we?"

"Tell me about yourself," I almost begged him. "I barely know anything about you."

He sighed and picked off a patch of candy floss, letting it dissolve on his tongue. "There's not much to tell you really."

"Well how old are you? What's your family like?"

"I'm eighteen," Jeremy started, then he looked down and a shadow of despair shrouded his face. "My family are pretty traditional, my parents and me and my brother."

"Why do you look so sad?" I asked, determined to find out something about him.

"I haven't been able to see any of them for a long time. I don't even know if he's okay." Jeremy looked up. "Tell me about your family."

We wandered side by side surrounded by the cheerfulness of those at the stalls and the games. I told Jeremy about my family and about my friends. I told him about my getting into university and my excitement to go somewhere new and meet new people.

"What course are you doing at university?" Jeremy asked. He seemed genuinely interested in everything I'd said. And the thought flashed through my mind that something was up. Teenage boys didn't listen the way Jeremy seemed to be. None that I had met anyway.

"Accounting," I admitted.

"Why accounting?"

"I think I would enjoy it," I said shyly. Most people didn't understand why I might be interested in such a dull job, but Jeremy didn't seem to judge me.

"Although, sometimes I wonder if I've made the right choice."

"What do you mean?" Jeremy asked me gently, as if I looked as unsure as I felt.

"I just wonder if I should really be rushing to go to university right now, or if this is really the job for me. Committing to so many years studying one thing, to realise that isn't the job I really want is a big concern. What if I don't enjoy it? I've never really tried to do anything else."

Jeremy nodded while he seemed to consider my words. "There's nothing to say whatever job you choose when you're eighteen you have to stick with for the rest of your life."

"I just feel like maybe I'm rushing into this." I hadn't discussed these feelings with anyone else, and telling Jeremy felt as though a weight was lifting off my back. I didn't know what had compelled me to talk about my concerns with someone I barely knew, but it was almost like the fact I hadn't known him long actually helped.

"If you really feel like this isn't what you want then you don't have to do it. But please don't let doubts get in the way of your life." The knowing in his eyes told me he was talking from some sort of experience and I longed to know what it was.

"I still plan to go to university. It is just a lot to think about."

"I'll miss hanging out with you while you're away," Jeremy said it quietly so I had to strain to hear him.

"I think I'll miss you too," I told him shyly. Was I really saying that to someone I had only just met? I'd known him little more than two nights and already I felt a strong pull towards him. Since Geore and I had broken up I had found it hard to have fun, but with Jeremy I had laughed a lot, and done things I wouldn't normally do. I would normally say no to visiting an amusement park, I would say no to the silly games and clearly fake fortune telling. He pushed me to try the stalls and to enjoy them. Jeremy was full of life.

"Good," he said. "I'm glad."

Everything seemed to shine brighter after that, the doubt I had felt about the park earlier that evening had vanished from my mind and I focused on enjoying the games.

I later found out Jeremy played a lot of basketball; this was after I witnessed him get every single ball through the hoops in a game that seemed to be made just for him.

I got the feeling Jeremy didn't like to reveal much about himself, but little things were beginning to come out in conversation. I found out that he was on a basketball team for many years but never made it to the final game of the season. He was a Scorpio, he loved sweets, he liked the colour green, he liked my short hair, and he really liked to have fun.

Whenever he realised he was talking too much about himself he started to deflect again and ask about me. I didn't mind really, it felt good to hear him opening up and not just playing games.

It was only an hour or so before the morning sun was due to rise when my eyes began to droop, and my limbs became too heavy to move. Two hours of sleep in forty-eight hours definitely wasn't the way to go. I tried to keep up with Jeremy's never-ending energy but soon found myself hanging onto his arm rather than walking by myself. I wasn't sure if Jeremy had noticed my dwindling energy but he wrapped his arm around mine and walked me to the entrance of the park.

With a deep sigh he released me and turned my face to his. "Do you have to go?" he asked sadly.

"I wish I could stay, but I need to get some sleep." A longing to stay with him and get to know him even more grew in my chest. "I'll come back." Something inside me told me he was someone worth knowing, I needed to listen to that voice and not let him go. I would come back again; I would come back every night if I had to.

The forest looked unfriendly that morning, like it was pushing me away from it, willing me to stay where I was. I could barely think about the walk home, through the difficult branches, only to sneak through the door and pray that neither of my parents would see me for the second morning in a row at some unspeakable time in the morning.

"I'll see you again tonight," I told him stubbornly sticking to the plan forming in my head.

Jeremy lifted his hand and stroked my cheek with the back of his soft fingers. "See you soon." With that he turned around and walked slowly back into the park. I kept my eyes on him until the crowds became too thick.

Finally, I gave in and turned back to the path to make my way home.

# Chapter 9

Black mist burdened my dreams as scenes of horror flashed through my consciousness. All the lights at the park were off leaving an almost grey colour to the machinery. It was empty with no one queuing for rides or buying sweets. Even Mrs. Millar stared at the ground with fear filling her eyes and twisting her eyebrows.

My numb feet took one step at a time until I was into the midst of the darkened wonderland. I noticed the roller coaster was broken and the pieces of the structure were bronze with rust just as it had been at the abandoned amusement park. How could that have happened when I had just been there a few hours before and it had been shiny and new and working just fine?

As my head turned, each of the tents, the games and buildings began to fall down and rot ate away at them, quickly turning them each into nothing more than piles of dirt.

Something caught my eye under the broken roller coaster. It was a body. Horror filled my bones and I bit back a scream as I hurried to the body, revealing what my aching heart had suspected. It was Jeremy. His body lay lifeless on the dead leaves with rotten dirt beneath him.

My legs could no longer hold my weight and I fell to his side, urgently searching his grey face for any signs of life.

Sweat seeped into the sheets under my body and a gasp escaped my lungs and my desperate eyes opened revealing nothing but my dark bedroom, as still and quiet as it usually was.

A dusting of uncertainty remained throughout my mind even as the dream faded away. Rapid heartbeats caused my breath to come out heavy and fast, feeling hot against my skin.

As the fog cleared and my heart settled my mind filled with different thoughts of the amusement park. Unlike the first night where everything felt murky and uncertain, after my second visit it was all clear, every memory remained. Most importantly I remembered Jeremy.

His overexcited grin flashed in my mind, and when I imagined looking into his beautiful eyes butterflies woke up in my stomach.

Realising I'd slept the day away I jumped out of bed and got ready for my next night at the park. I made myself a quick dinner, seeing my parents only briefly in passing.

"I would have offered you dinner with us but you were still asleep when we ate," Mum said, concern flashing across her face. Avoiding the obvious question in her voice I told her it was fine and ate in my room.

As I sat on my bed with my legs crossed and my dinner plate in my lap, my phone began to vibrate next to me. I had barely looked at my phone over the last few days. Messages had been popping up on the screen but for some reason, I just didn't want to read them.

Answering Jayne's call with a cheery "hello" I sat back and listened to her immediate rant.

"Hey, are you okay? I haven't heard from you much recently; you haven't replied to any of my messages. I know it's only been two days, but we usually text a lot throughout the day so I just wanted to make sure..." Jayne's voice came out rushed and breathless as if she'd been holding that in for a while.

"I'm sorry, I just haven't been looking at my phone much recently," I told her reassuringly.

"Well, the guys are all coming to mine tonight if you want to come over. We're just going to put a film on," she told me.

I did want to go over. Staying in and watching movies was more my thing than traipsing through dark woodland in the middle of the night, but I wouldn't be able to see Jeremy if I went over to Jayne's that evening.

"I can't tonight," I told her, without giving her any other details.

There was a pause on the other side of the phone call and then a long sigh came through to my ear. "Is this about the other night?" Jayne asked me, a sad tone in her voice. "Look, I'm sorry about saying you were boring. I really didn't mean anything by it. I think I was just a bit hyped up about it being the start of summer."

The memory of our little spat had all but left my mind, its place filled with thoughts of someone else. Assuring Jayne that wasn't the case,

I told her I just had plans with my parents that evening. It wasn't completely unbelievable.

"So, we're alright then?" Jayne asked nervously.

"Really, it's fine," I told her, desperate for this conversation to be over. It was rare that Jayne and I argued, and the apologies and making up part of the argument was the worst part in my opinion. I would rather just sweep it under the rug and never mention it again.

"Well, how about tomorr –" Jayne began as I tried to hang up, telling her I had to get back to my parents.

Guilt flashed through me as I finished off my dinner and applied some makeup to my now rested face. Ready to see Jeremy for a third night – it was starting to feel like an addiction.

# Chapter 10

"Why are you always here?" I asked Jeremy. We sat facing each other on the ground, between two stalls where no one would be walking. That night when I'd arrived, I'd decided I didn't want to play games, I wanted to spend time with Jeremy, and get to know him even more. I was still unsure why he chose to spend every night at the amusement park and not out somewhere else.

"I can't leave," he said, matter-of-factly. He wore the same clothes for the third day in a row, and I wondered if they were perhaps the only clothes he owned, they didn't look dirty from excessive wear but maybe he washed them every day.

"Why not?" I asked, thinking this was some kind of joke. "Can't think of anywhere better to spend your time?"

"This is just where I stay." Once again he spoke as if everything he said was completely normal. How could I question such assuredness?

"You live in the amusement park?"

I took a sip of my drink. That night Jeremy had introduced me to a Magical Milkshake. A galaxy of blues and greens swirled around the plastic cup, glitter like stars flashed from inside the drink when the lights around us caught it. Mrs. Millar hadn't looked too impressed when we walked past her stand without stopping for any of her sweet treats, but then, she never looked too impressed when she saw me.

"I guess you could say that," Jeremy agreed.

"Don't you ever want to leave?"

"Why would I? It is so fun here," he laughed as if my question was ridiculous.

A group of teenage boys crowded around the stall I leant against and I was able to catch a peek at a couple of them. They looked familiar and I realised that I recognised them from the first night I had visited Jeremy's Amusement Park. They cheered boyishly as if someone had won the game and received their toy prize. They shuffled around to let the boy on the side get to the middle for his turn and a new boy took position in my view.

A boyish chuckle vibrated through the group and they all compared their stuffed animal prizes, throwing them at each other in a short-lived war. Soon they were picking toys up off the ground and setting off to their next match elsewhere.

I was sure I'd seen them have this exact same war the night before. Did they play this same game every night just to chuck teddies at each other?

Jeremy's eyes were watching me curiously when I turned back to face him. I looked down at my lap where I held the raspberry flavoured milkshake and then back up to see he was still looking at me.

"What are you looking at?" I asked, a hot blush rising in my cheeks.

"I was just thinking how beautiful you are," he said seriously as if the thought had just occurred to him.

As much as I tried to prevent it, I just couldn't stop the smile from spreading across my cheeks. I held his stare this time and a grin grew on his face as well. Could anyone ever get tired of that grin?

Finding my gaze drop to his plump lips I wondered what they would feel like against mine.

Jeremy kept his gaze on me while we chatted in our private seating in between the games. We talked more about my university course and I told him all the options you had as an accountant, all the ways you could help people and businesses.

I soon began to notice that the more I talked to him about my university plans the more he seemed to dismiss them, telling me that "university isn't really that important". I couldn't tell what had caused the change in him; he had seemed to be encouraging me the previous night, but now I got the impression he didn't want me to go at all. I was feeling more unsure about my decision than ever.

"If you could have any job in the world, what would it be?" I asked Jeremy, curious as to what he planned for his future.

He thought on the question for a while before answering. "For a while I wanted to be a professor or a teacher." I was surprised by his answer, realising how little I really knew about him.

"Why don't you anymore?"

"It wouldn't be possible now," Jeremy sighed.

"Why not? You could still do it," I encouraged him enthusiastically. "What made you want to be a teacher in the first place?"

"It seemed like an important role. To play a part in the shaping future generations – it could be really great." Jeremy's smile began to come back slowly as he talked. I could tell something had happened to stop this dream of his but he seemed passionate about it.

Jeremy told me how his uncle had been a teacher. It had been his uncle who helped him and his brother with homework and projects. He talked about his uncle as if he was no longer around and I couldn't bring myself to ask what had happened to him.

"He sounds like a great man," I said.

"What about you?" Jeremy asked. "Any family members that inspire you?"

This was a question that was always asked at school, especially when we were being encouraged to decide on a career and life path. Who inspires you and why?

"My parents," I admitted. I was probably the only teenager I knew who had respect for their parents. That's not to say we didn't fight and disagree on a lot of things. "It's not like they've really had it particularly hard or had to overcome anything major, they're just always there for me," I explained to Jeremy.

"Parents like that are hard to find."

"Were your parents not there for you?"

"It's not that they didn't try," Jeremy told me. "They just got busy and distracted a lot. It was just my brother and me most of the time." A sadness came over him again and all I wanted was to make him happy, to solve all his problems just to see his smile and hear his laugh.

"Sounds like the perfect partnership."

"It was." Jeremy nodded, trying not to lose his smile again.

"Tell me about your brother," I said.

"Not tonight," Jeremy replied. Before I could protest he announced that we should go on a ride before the night ended.

Jeremy led me towards a ride that I hadn't noticed before, the teacups, with their large, colourful, cup-shaped seats that spun around. It wasn't the ride I'd expected him to choose.

We took our seat in a blue teacup with white polka dots covering the outside of it, next to several other groups in the other five patterned cups around our own. The seats were surprisingly comfy with a squishy leather pillow covering the full length of the seat.

Next to us was another couple, older than most I had seen that evening. They were perhaps in their late thirties. They looked at each other with such tenderness I almost felt as though they should be somewhere much more private. I longed for someone to look at me that way.

We put our hands on the holder in the middle and felt the cup begin to move, slowly circling round and round until everything around us was a blur of colours and voices.

Music sang around us as we smiled at each other, I wondered if one day Jeremy would look at me the way the couple beside us looked at each other. Children shouted their joy from another one of the cups as their parents encouraged them, calling out with them as their cup moved.

Allowing my curious eyes to lock tightly onto Jeremy's as we sat almost opposite each other, I watched as he glanced over my face, taking in every detail, lingering just for a moment on my lips, and then meeting my gaze again. His grin tugged at the corners of his mouth but he didn't show his teeth to me, instead he just watched me, mirroring my own observation of him.

Before I knew it the ride was over and all the other people were exiting their teacups. Staying in my seat I watched Jeremy to see what he would do next. He glanced up at the sky behind me and then with a sad smile his eyes found mine again. I'd been so captivated watching Jeremy I hadn't even noticed the sun was already on the rise. It would be daylight before I arrived home.

"I should go," I said sadly.

"Why do you have to go? Can't you just stay here... with me?" Jeremy took my hand and held me in place.

For a moment my mind went fuzzy, and I searched it for an answer. Why couldn't I just stay? I knew there had to be something stopping me from spending all my time there, and for that reason I insisted I had to go.

"I want you to stay," Jeremy said, a little more forcefully than I'd ever seen him before.

"I'll be back tomorrow." I tugged gently at my arm until he released it.

As I walked through the forest, I wondered if leaving the park that morning had been a mistake.

# Chapter 11

The next night as I approached the entrance of Jeremy's Amusement Park, I stopped and turned my face towards the sky. The bright stars seemed to be closer than normal, glittering down at me.

"Mae, what are you doing out here?" Jeremy asked as he came to join me, wearing the same clothes again.

"Aren't the stars beautiful? Do they always look like this here?" I asked him as he took my hand and led me into the park without so much as a glance at the sky.

"I guess," he replied. His dismissal disappointed me and I wondered if he even realised what a beautiful and lively place he spent his time in.

Before I knew it Jeremy had led me to the first game I had played at the park, the one with water balloons and darts. I wondered to myself if he ever got bored playing the same games over and over again.

My skills had not improved since the last time we played, although that time at least I had popped one balloon on my turn.

After a while of playing games with little conversation between us I decided I wanted to hear his voice again, I wanted to hear him talk about himself.

"What school do you go to?" I asked him slowly, cautious of the fact he didn't seem to like talking about himself.

"I've finished school now," he replied without turning my way.

"Okay, so what school did you go to? We're the same age but I don't recognise you."

With a long sigh Jeremy said, "Do we have to talk about me tonight? Can't we just have fun?"

I was taken aback and a little hurt by his response. "Well, isn't the point in us hanging out to get to know each other? Don't you want to get to know me?"

I could see Jeremy take a deep breath and force a smile onto his face. "Of course, I do," he said, cupping my face with his hand and looking deep into my eyes. "But as we're here, I thought it would be nice to play some games for a while."

Unwelcome doubt began to creep in. "Well, what about tomorrow? You could come into town and we could talk some more."

"I can't leave here," he told me gently, his soft hand remained under my chin.

"I'm sure they could handle this place without you for one day?" I reasoned with him.

He whipped his hand back from my face and turned away. "I just can't, Mae."

Can't or won't? I thought to myself angrily. I tried to squash the doubt and hurt I was feeling towards Jeremy.

Suddenly, his beautiful bright grin spread across his face. He suggested we go somewhere else, play some other games and once his hand was on the small of my back, leading me away, I just couldn't resist doing what he said. A warmth spread through me once again but underneath it was the doubt that had begun to take root in my stomach.

For the rest of the evening, I found myself watching his every movement, taking in every word he said, feeling every time he touched me. I wasn't sure what it was exactly that felt off but I couldn't deny that he wasn't as perfect as I'd originally thought. Determined not to let these new queries ruin my night I allowed myself to have fun with him. I deserved to have fun with a man again.

I couldn't stop myself from wondering what George would say if Jayne told him about Jeremy, what he would do if he saw us together at the amusement park, with Jeremy's arm wrapped around me while he helped me aim.

I shook my head and focused my mind again on Jeremy and the joy flashing in his eyes.

Jeremy held my hand as we wandered to the forest so I could once again leave him at the amusement park. When we reached the point where he normally turned back, her turned to face me and leant his head close to mine, placing a tender kiss on my cheek.

Although the kiss hatched butterflies in my stomach, I couldn't help but feel disappointed that it hadn't been on my lips. How did he see me? As a friend? As a sister? I desperately hoped that soon he would want more.

# Chapter 12

Warmth swam over my skin as I made my way home in the morning sunshine. The summer was off to a hot start and I couldn't help but feel a little disappointed at my new schedule of sleeping all day and going out all night. People were already rising as I entered the town, cafes were turning their signs to open.

As I passed a large clear window someone waved frantically from their seat at the table inside. I didn't quite recognise them so I assumed the waving was meant for someone else. I ignored it and carried on walking. Whatever had taken over my mind at the amusement park was apparently still creating a fog in my memories and I didn't even recognise my best friend's voice.

"Mae!" Jayne called my name as she ran out of the cafe. I turned slowly to see her expectant face coming straight for me and the image of her and the rest of my life became clear once again. "Where have you been?"

"What do you mean?" I said, wondering how she knew I had been out all night.

"I've been calling you all morning, and yesterday." She sounded exasperated as she took my arm in hers, leading me back to the cafe she had come from.

I patted my pockets looking for my phone before remembering I'd left it at home. I'd been so distracted the last few days I hadn't even thought about my phone or who might be trying to contact me. "I must've left it at home."

"Well, it doesn't matter now, we're all getting breakfast."

I spotted Tommy, Adam and George seated around a large table in front of the window. Accepting that I was now joining them I put on my best polite smile.

When George's eyes met mine I suddenly worried what I might look like. I had dressed casually last night in an outfit that I hoped would show off the right curves, but after hours of wear I feared my make up may now be smudged under my eyes and my hair a mess.

I excused myself to the bathroom before taking a seat at their table. I let a deep breath fill my lungs and then let it out slowly before taking a glance in the cafe's bathroom mirror. It was well lit with a long window above the mirror and white walls.

My short pixie cut hair was only a little messy and I used my fingers to flatten out the tangles and neaten up my fringe. I let a small drop of water land on a tissue and wiped under my eyes for any dark patches of fallen mascara. Finally, I applied a layer of lip balm before making my way back to the table.

"They took our order while you were gone so I ordered you a breakfast," Jayne informed me.

"Thanks, did you order a coffee?" I tried not to sound too desperate.

"Of course," she smirked, well aware of me and my coffee habits.

"You're amazing, thank you." I sat at the end of the table with Jayne to my right. From my seat I had a good view for people watching on the street outside. With George sitting directly opposite me I needed somewhere else to look, so the window was the perfect distraction.

When our drinks arrived, I gratefully accepted my coffee and took a big sip straight away.

"Tired?" George questioned; he was looking at me quizzically. For months every time he'd looked at me, I'd longed for it to be in the same way he used to, when we were together and he could make me feel special. Now I just wished it was Jeremy sitting opposite.

"No," I said defensively. "It's just good coffee."

Jayne swished her long golden locks into my face multiple times as she turned constantly to talk to the whole table at once, even getting a few strands in my drink. I scooched my chair to the side to try and avoid the firing line. Tommy was lucky he could put his arm around her and hold her too close for her hair to fly around him.

Adam held back a laugh as he watched me struggling to politely get out of her way, my eyes caught his and I rolled them sarcastically and we both smirked at each other. Luckily when the food arrived, she sat still long enough for me to get through my meal without any strands of hair landing in my food.

With three milkshakes swirling around in my stomach from the evening at Jeremy's Amusement Park I was grateful for some solid food to soak it all up.

"So, what do you guys want to do with the rest of the summer?" Jayne asked the table.

Everyone looked around at each other hoping for someone to answer. Clearly no one had planned for that question. Jayne was always one for over planning everything she did.

"Let's just hang out this summer," Tommy suggested. "Take it easy before the hard work starts."

"What do you mean?" Jayne demanded. "We only have a couple of months until we're all separated, we need to do something fun."

"Well as you just said we have months to do something, we don't need to find something monumental to do right now," I reasoned with her.

Jayne didn't appear to have the same hope for university as the rest of us, she was going because she wanted the education, but if it was up to her, she would've had us all in the same university, and living in the same accommodation.

A strip of light lay across my outstretched arm on the table, so hot I thought it could burn if I left my arm there for long enough. I noticed George also looking until her noticed me watching and quickly looked away.

I removed my arm and instead glanced out the window to the street outside. It was still early and shops were only now opening. A few women walked past in similar smart skirts and blouses, probably all on their way to wherever it was they worked together. They had matching straight hairstyles tied back into neat ponytails.

Across the road was an elderly couple walking with their arms linked. They had just emerged from the bakery and were carrying a small bag of freshly baked goods. The man was hunched with a walking stick and the woman stepped slowly so her partner could keep to her pace. I wondered if when I was their age, I would have someone to go to the bakery with me, someone who would wait for me if I needed a walking stick.

"Well, if you guys want to play games then Mae can come back to mine and we can make the most of the sun in the garden," Jayne was saying as I reentered the conversation. Once again, I was being volunteered into things without being asked. But it was about time I got a bit of sun on my barely tanned skin, so I agreed with Jayne and we all made our separate ways for the day.

# Chapter 13

Jayne lived in the opposite direction to my house from the cafe where we'd eaten breakfast, and it took twice as long to walk there than if we'd gone to mine. Luckily the sun was a glorious companion on our journey. I shimmied off my thin knit cardigan leaving me in just a flowery vest. Jayne was wearing loose white shorts with a vest to match and sandals that slapped the bottom of her feet every time she took a step.

The garden at Jayne's parents' house was almost bigger than the house itself. A large wooden decking was built at the top with a round outdoor table and two lounge chairs. Jayne often moved these two chairs to the bottom of the garden where the sun could reach them at almost any time of day.

Their house was lucky to only have one neighbor on the left-hand side, the rest of the house had no obstructing views at all and looked right over a long stretch of hill-side. The best view was from the upstairs balcony. I often thought if it were my house I would build a comfy seating area on it so I could spend all my time there. It was Jayne's parent's bedroom balcony unfortunately, so we couldn't made use of it even if we wanted to.

I helped Jayne move the lounge chairs to the bottom of the garden and waited for her to retrieve the long, thick cushions that covered them.

Just as I was trying to hide a yawn she came back into the garden with the cushions, spotting my dirty secret straight away.

"Tired already?" she asked. "What's keeping you awake at night? Or should I say who?"

I shook my head and willed the blush I could feel to go away. "No one, it's just been a long few days."

We settled into the comfy lounge chairs and directed ourselves to where the sun would best reach our bodies.

"So, you didn't see him again? The guy you said you met the other night when you disappeared?"

I wondered if it was wise to tell Jayne about Jeremy, she had a habit of not keeping secrets. But why did it need to be a secret? I admitted to myself that the circumstances were a little weird to explain to someone who had not been to the amusement park and had not met Jeremy. There were things I still couldn't explain and didn't understand. Part of me hoped that she would gossip a little with the guys in the group, if only so George would know I had been talking to someone new. I knew I shouldn't worry about what he thought of me or who I might be spending time with, but some part of me wasn't over him yet and I wanted him to think I was moving on.

"I did see him again actually," I admitted.

"I knew it," she exclaimed. "Go on then, tell me everything!"

Jayne rolled eagerly onto her side to face me and fully concentrate on what I had to say. I didn't tell her everything, I knew she wouldn't understand and wouldn't care about the small things.

First, I told her about Jeremy, trying not to sound too infatuated over him as I described his perfect features and playful nature. I told her about his caring and enthusiastic personality. I described in great detail the beauty of his eyes and the way the blue changed in different lights but no matter what shade they were I found it hard to look away.

Then, I told her how he had taken me to an amusement park, telling her that it was so far to walk that I was sure it was close to the next town over, but that walking there with him had been enchanting. I didn't mention how after that first trip there I didn't seem to have to walk at all, somehow, I just seemed to appear at the entrance of the amusement park and when I left I would just open my eyes and be at the abandoned amusement park, as if there was no journey between the two. I didn't tell her about the strange things I'd noticed, like the same people showing up every night in the same clothes they'd worn every night previously, and the fact that the roller coaster was dangerous and yet people were still riding it, and how Jeremy refused to leave.

Jayne was ecstatic for me, squealing at every detail I gave her and encouraging me to tell her more.

"He sounds amazing," she said when I finally finished. I agreed with her, trying to play it cool as if talking about him wasn't filling me with even more fluttering feelings for him. "You haven't even told me his name yet."

"Jeremy," I said quietly. Somehow it felt like saying it out loud would ruin it. Jayne squealed again, informing me that was a good name. I wasn't sure what made a name good or bad.

We lay peacefully for a while as Jayne soaked in the information I had just filled her with and I let myself feel the warmth, not only from the sun but from the feelings I had for Jeremy.

Jayne chuckled to herself. "Isn't it a weird coincidence that what brought you together with this guy that keeps taking you to an amusement park is the fact that we were exploring an old amusement park because we heard someone died there?"

I had completely forgotten about the small fact of someone dying. The dark feelings I had forgotten about from the nightmare I'd had the day before were growing in my stomach now. I had no idea why what Jayne said made me nervous, but something felt wrong.

"I guess it's a little weird," I said.

"I wonder how he really died and if anyone else was hurt," she said, her mood clearly not as affected by this topic as mine. Just the thought of it made my pulse race. "What do you think his name was?"

I felt a weight suddenly fall on me as if my lack of sleep and sudden anxiety mixed together to tie me down. Thinking about someone dying, especially after the dream I'd had was too much for me. I had to get out of there.

I didn't look at Jayne as I ran up her garden, through her house and out her front door, I just shouted behind me. "I have to go."

# Chapter 14

I could barely look at any of the passersby as I practically ran all the way home. Sweat was building on my neck as the sun glared down upon me.

What had come over me so suddenly? It was as if merly talking about Jeremy made me need to be with him, to see him and talk to him and touch him. Then the reminder of seeing his dead body in my dreams had changed my thoughts completely. It didn't make any sense. I must have been more tired than I thought.

"Oof!" Someone grunted as I slammed right into them. "Watch where you're going."

"Sorr –" I looked up to see an annoyed Mrs. Millar looking down at me, her hands on her round hips as she waited for her apology.

Her eyes seemed to have crinkled even more around the edges since I had seen her last and her hair was now more silver than red. Her fun, colourful amusement park uniform was gone and she wore jeans and a summery blouse. It looked strange on her, as if she shouldn't be in the real world, she belonged in the world of the amusement park. She didn't seem to recognise me and yet she looked just as unhappy as she had when she saw me at Jeremy's Amusement Park.

"Mrs. Millar?" I said, unable to think of anything else.

"Do I know you?" she said, lifting one curious eyebrow to inspect my face.

"I saw you at the amusement park," I said. "With Jeremy."

Her face lightened and a sad sort of pity filled it instead. "I'm so sorry, it's been a long time since I worked there. It was very sad what happened to your friend."

A long time, I repeated to myself. But I had seen her just last night. Maybe I hadn't, maybe it was a different Mrs. Millar I had seen. Sisters perhaps. "You know him?"

"Only a little, he often came to my stall when he came to the park. He was always causing mischief but he took a break for his sweets."

Mischief? "What was your stall?" I asked, already knowing what she would say.

"Handmade sweets," she said proudly. "Best sweets around if I do say so myself."

I couldn't speak. I left Mrs. Millar on the street and carried on walking home. I couldn't take the pity she was sending my way. What had happened to Jeremy? I'd seen him only last night, surely this was some kind of joke.

The image of Jeremy's lifeless body from my dream flashed before my eyes, he was laying under the roller coaster. The thought of losing Jeremy filled me with terror. Tears stung the back of my eyes. This couldn't be true; how could it be? It was only a dream.

By the time I made it back to my house I was running, sweat dripped from my face but an undeniable urge to know the truth overcame me, blinding me from seeing any of my surroundings. I didn't check if my parents were home or where they were, I just let myself in and ran up the stairs to my room.

"Mae," Mum called through my closed door. "Can I come in?"

"No," I called back, wiping away the tears that were streaming down my cheeks. I didn't even know why I was crying. I didn't know that anything had happened to him. "I'm changing," I lied. I took a few deep breaths to steady myself.

"Are you okay?" She sounded concerned.

"I'm fine," I said. What could I say? I couldn't tell her what was going on.

After a moment, I heard her soft footsteps retreating back downstairs and I curled my body tightly on top of my bed.

When my body stopped shaking and my tears dried up, I came to a decision. I couldn't wait until this evening, I had to go to Jeremy's Amusement Park now.

By now I could find my way to the abandoned amusement park with my eyes closed, which I may as well have done as it was always so dark when I went. That day, however, the sun was high in the clear sky and the path was well lit, there were even a few people that passed me on the path before I stepped away into the thick trees.

It looked different during the day, the large hazardous roots were easy to step over and the branches didn't seem to come for me quite as much as usual. Even in the thick forest small beams of sunlight pierced through the leaves.

There was no one at the abandoned amusement park and I made my way straight across to the broken wall where the path to Jeremy's Amusement Park began. I wondered what it would look like during the day. Would the lights all be turned off? Would anyone even be there?

I took a long step into the forest, and then another step and then another step. This was when I would usually open my eyes to see the park in front of me. All I could see then was more of the forest, filled with shadows and disappointment.

I walked further into the forest, slowly at first and then faster and faster until I was sprinting, desperate to find Jeremy and his amusement park. The forest seemed to go on forever and with no end in sight I slowed down to catch my breath. I had no idea how far I had gone, it felt like miles, but surely if I was that far in, I should have found it already.

Suddenly, an uncomfortable thought filled me with worry; what if it was no longer there?

No, I told myself. Where would it have gone? I must have just gone the wrong way, everything looked different during the day, it would have been easy to mistake one path for another. I decided I would come back that night to confront Jeremy and find out the truth.

It was late afternoon by the time I had found my way back out of the vast forest. After running for a long time and not paying attention to which way I went, it took a long time to locate the place I had entered. Eventually, I found myself back at the old, rusty park. Exhaustion took over me, once again, and I felt myself wobbling as I walked home, glistening spots surrounded my vision until I finally arrived at my house and collapsed on my bed into a deep dark sleep.

# Chapter 15

When my dry eyes creaked open it was still light outside. I reached for my phone to discover I had slept all night and half of the day. It was already two pm and I had missed a night with Jeremy. A dreadful longing overcame me as I realised I would have to wait even longer to see him.

Heaving myself out of bed, I crept down stairs and into the kitchen for a big glass of refreshing water, before stepping into the living room where my dad was reading the newspaper. I took the seat next to him and let out a sigh.

"Gah!" Dad gasped. "Mae, you made me jump. I didn't see you come downstairs."

"Sorry," I said.

His face turned serious. "Are you okay? You're looking a little pale."

"I'm fine, just a little tired."

"Perhaps you should stop going out so late then." It wasn't often that Dad did the serious conversations, he usually left those for my mum. But something must have made him worry enough to say what he was thinking.

I stayed quiet until he lifted his newspaper back in front of his face. I couldn't tell him that anything was going to change; that was something I just couldn't guarantee.

A groggy tiredness slowed down my aching legs as I made my way back to the park that night. I shivered from a chill making its way down my spine while I looked at the forest ahead of me.

With a deep breath I took a step into the forest and towards the amusement park. Lights flashed before my eyes and cheers filled my ears. Relief flushed my body and I ran to the entrance of the park where Jeremy always met me. But he wasn't there. My desperate eyes searched the park for his brilliant smile, listening intently for his laugh.

"You shouldn't have come back," the ticket woman croaked from where she sat at her table just as she did every night. "You let him down."

"Where is he?" I asked her, a little unnerved. The thought of upsetting Jeremy filled me with regret, and I had to remind myself that I had come for answers.

Without a word the ticket woman pursed her thin lips and looked down the table. Accepting I would get no answers from her I continued further into the park. None of the other attendees seemed to notice the resentment seeping from the workers.

I knew Jeremy was friendly with each of the staff members but from the glares I received from each of them I realised that he must be very close with the whole park, and they must all care deeply for him.

An itch formed on my bare neck. Mrs. Millar, I thought to myself. Turning around I instantly spotted her scowl on the other side of the park. As uncomfortable as she made me feel I knew she could tell me where Jeremy was.

"I didn't think we would see you again," she growled. A shadow seemed to settle around us and the laughter and talking faded away. This Mrs. Millar's face appeared to have softened around the edges, the wrinkles were less defined than in the woman I had met on the street outside Jayne's house. It must have been the lights that made her appear younger than she had in the street. "Perhaps it would have been better if you hadn't returned."

I swallowed the fear she lit inside me and replaced it with determination. "Where's Jeremy?"

"Silly girl," Mrs. Millar scoffed. "He doesn't want to see you."

"It was an accident!" I insisted. "I didn't mean to sleep for so long."

Mrs. Millar seemed to grow taller in the moment, towering over me as if I were nothing to her but a miniscule ant on the ground.

"Mae," Jeremy's soft voice whispered from behind me. Mrs. Millar deflated back to her regular size and the surrounding sounds and light returned.

Angry from talking to Mrs. Millar I spun around, ready to protest my innocence. The betrayal in Jeremy's eyes stopped me in my stride. The deep blue seemed to have faded slightly and the spring in his step seemed to be broken.

"Where were you?" he asked sadly. "I waited all night for you."

"I tried to find you yesterday, during the day. But I couldn't find the park" I told him.

"You said you would come back at midnight."

"I'm sorry, I fell asleep." Reaching for his hand, I tried to make him understand that I hadn't deliberately neglected him. He pulled it away, out of my reach.

"Don't you care about me?" he asked.

"Of course, I do! It won't happen again, Jeremy. I promise."

His face softened. "You promise?" he asked.

"Yes, Jeremy. I promise."

He took my hand at last and relief flooded through me. I didn't know what I would have done if he'd stayed angry with me.

"I knew you wouldn't leave me," he said, leading me back to Mrs. Millar's stall, where her disapproving face glared down at me.

Silver strands seemed to shimmer in the moonlight from on top of her head exaggerating the frightful glint in her eyes.

Jeremy seemed to think intensely about what to eat, considering all options and weighing out the pros and cons. "I want to make the right choice," Jeremy explained when he noticed me smirking at his indecision.

Finally, he made a decision and bought a bag of colourful gummy sweets, passing me a bag of my own. But he didn't take me somewhere to sit and enjoy my sweets, instead he decided we would play games while we ate. We had already played most of the games on my first few visits, so we had another go at each of them before moving onto a new one.

The game he chose involved throwing tennis balls at bottles stacked in sixes. If Jeremy hadn't already realised how bad my aim was, he would soon find out with that game. The man behind the booth giving us instructions had a loud, commanding voice, booming from behind his thick brown beard. His eyebrows were bushy with flecks of grey, above his large dark eyes.

I threw my first tennis ball and missed the stack altogether. "You can do better than that!" the man laughed. Jeremy knocked down the whole stack in one throw and I envied his effortless talent for amusement park games.

"You can do it," Jeremy encouraged me, stroking my arm as he spoke.

I took a deep breath and aimed again for the white bottles. I threw the ball and watched as it flew forward and took out a stack of bottles.

"I did it!" I jumped up and wrapped my arms around Jeremy in an excited hug. I soaked in his warmth against my body and felt his strong arms hold me against him.

"You're getting better," Jeremy laughed. He loosened his hold on me and I leant back to look in his eyes. He lifted his hand and ran his fingers through my hair. "I'm so happy you're here, Mae."

My cheeks burnt. "Me too," I said. I couldn't stop my eyes from slipping down slowly to his plump, inviting lips. Part of me wished he would act on my desire. Part of me wished I had the confidence to make the first move.

Moving on to the next game of the night I stood slightly to the side and just observed Jeremy throwing basketballs in nets at various distances from us. The thick muscle in his upper arms flexed as he pulled the ball back and aimed strategically at the goals. Leaving his arm outstretched as the ball flew through the air, he waited for it to land perfectly in the net furthest away.

Watching the light in his eyes as he enjoyed winning yet another game, I wondered if it was winning he enjoyed more than the game itself.

"Do you miss playing basketball on a team?" I asked him curiously.

"I suppose I do sometimes," Jeremy admitted.

"Why did you quit?"

"I just couldn't play anymore," Jeremy said, in that way I had grown used to, that meant he wouldn't be going into any more detail.

"Do you miss your teammates?" I continued, still curious about his life.

"To be honest I wasn't really that close to my team. They were great to play with but outside of that we had nothing in common."

I seemed to often find myself surprised by Jeremy's answers and the small details of his life that he shared with me.

"What are your friends like, then?" I asked. I imagined Jeremy and a group of friends in the library or sixth form common room working on assignments together while also laughing and enjoying their free periods at school.

"Not much to tell really, they aren't that interesting," Jeremy said casually.

"What do you mean? Don't you have any friends?" The images in my head began to change and I began to see Jeremy by himself in the common room, nodding as people he sort of knew from his classes walked past.

"Of course, I have friends, they just aren't that interesting to talk about. They don't do a lot."

A new image emerged in my mind of Jeremy and a group of misfits disrupting classes and messing around, throwing things in the common room annoying other students. I couldn't imagine Jeremy fitting in with that group. He had told me about his ambition to become a teacher and I wondered if that ambition had been further in his past than he implied. Could the persona I imagined for him be so far wrong?

A sudden uninvited thought crossed my mind and I wondered whether if I had known Jeremy in school we would have been friends.

"We haven't got long before morning," Jeremy sighed.

Spending the last few hours with Jeremy had made me completely forget all about my other life. I felt as though I was only just beginning to get to know the real him and I wanted to stay and talk to him for longer, to experience everything he experienced.

A pulling feeling reminded me that I had to leave. There was something waiting for me outside the park, I just couldn't remember what.

"Why don't you stay this time?" Jeremy asked, as if reading my mind.

"I... I can't," I said, still unsure why that was.

Jeremy's eyebrows pulled together and he frowned at me. "Fine," he said.

"I'll see you tomorrow," I called to him as I left the park.

"Okay," he said, half-heartedly.

# Chapter 16

As I walked home that morning, my mind filled with thoughts of Jeremy. Had he truly forgiven me? His behavior had been different, almost childish in a bad way, rather than his normal excitable state. I suddenly wondered what Jayne and the others would make of him. Would he seem so special if I wasn't alone with him? I shook my head, of course he would. I felt guilty even questioning my feelings for him. The one thing I knew for sure was that I couldn't miss another night with him. I hated upsetting him like that.

When I thought of how I would have to leave for university at the end of the summer a knot took hold of my stomach. How would I go so long during term time without seeing him?

For a moment I wondered if he would come with me, but that thought quickly disappeared when I remembered how much he loved his theme park. He'd never give that up for me. Or would he? Could I ask that of him?

Before I could think of anything else, I needed to get some sleep. I climbed into bed as soon as I arrived home, avoiding seeing my parents as they began getting ready for their day. Several times I was woken up by the worries filling my stomach, and I pulled the duvet tight around my body to force myself back to sleep.

Finally, mid-afternoon, I decided it was time to give up with my attempts to get some rest and just get up to enjoy a few hours of sunlight, something I had all but forgotten about since visiting Jeremy.

I decided to take the rest of the afternoon for myself. It hadn't been long since I had met Jeremy but I felt as though I'd spent that whole time either with him or losing sleep over him.

Ignoring the deep, dark bags surrounding my eyes when I looked in the mirror I got into a nice summer dress, and made myself comfortable in a green plastic garden chair, the sun warming my skin comfortably as I sipped on an iced lemonade. This was the kind of relaxation I'd expected to have over my last summer holiday before university. Lots of people in my year were working and saving what they could, but I'd decided on a different route.

A tall wooden fence surrounded our small square garden, just high enough to stop people looking in but not high enough to block the midday sun. The grass was warm and tough between my toes and I reveled in the normality of the afternoon relaxation. It had been ages since anything had felt normal.

Delicious fresh air filled my lungs, I held it there for a few seconds before letting it out in one big smooth rush. Cars drove on the main road far enough away that I could only just hear them and instead listened to the musical chirping coming from trees at the front of the house. I often saw a robin hunting in the small flower patch my mum had planted at the bottom of the garden.

I soaked up the glorious warmth of the sun until the late afternoon when I heard my parents arriving home from work. Surprise crossed their faces as they saw me coming into the house from the garden. I told them how I'd spent the day sunbathing and they told me about work.

I offered to help cook dinner but my mum told me to take a seat at the table while she put something together.

"Mae," she said as she chopped vegetables. "How are you?"

"What do you mean?"

"It's just that we've not seen you much recently, and I've heard you sneaking out late and sneaking back in the early hours. And then you're in your room sleeping all through the day, but you still look exhausted. We're just worried about you."

I sighed deeply, my attempts at sneaking around obviously hadn't worked. "I'm fine, Mum. Just having some fun before uni, that's all."

"I ran into Jayne this morning and she asked about you. She said she'd barely seen you. I had assumed you were out with your friends."

I didn't know how to answer that so I looked down at my hands on the table as my mum carried on.

"I know you're eighteen now, but I can still worry about you."

"I know, Mum, I'm sorry," I told her truthfully.

"Is it a boy?" It always came down to this question. Every time mum talked to me, she would find a way to ask me about boys, assuming everything I did with my time was under the influence of boys.

I hated to admit that this time she was right. "Sort of."

"Are you back together with George?" I didn't need the reminder of how disappointed she had been when George and I had broken up.

"No, Mum, it's someone else."

She looked concerned as she used her knife to slide the vegetables off the chopping board and into the frying pan. "Okay, Mae."

Stifling a yawn, I decided to confide in my mum. We'd always had a good relationship with each other, even if usually I chose not to fill her in too much on the details of my life. When I did give her the odd details, I could tell it made her happy to know more about me.

"Mum?" I said. "Are you happy with your life?"

She looked a bit taken back by the question. "Of course, I am, why would you ask that?"

"I just mean, do you ever wish you had done something else?"

She stopped stirring the dinner, turned off the hob and came to sit next to me at the table. "Of course, I've considered how my life might have gone if I had chosen a different route. But whenever I picture how things might have turned out, this life is definitely the life I want to be in."

I nodded thoughtfully.

"What is this about?"

"I guess I've just been wondering recently if I'm making the right life choice."

My mum took a deep breath while she pondered over how to respond. She tucked a loose strand of her hazelnut hair behind her ear, showing off the rose coloured studs she had in. "I think," she started, "I think that only you can answer that. What do you want to do? If you picture yourself in thirty years and that's not where you want to be, then change the path you're on."

It sounded logical when she said it like that, but how could I know really where I'd be in thirty years? I could drop out of university in a year and end up somewhere completely different or I could graduate and have a very successful life. I couldn't know how I would feel a year from now or thirty years from now. I supposed maybe that was the point. Maybe I just had to do what felt right and if it stopped feeling right change paths.

"Thanks, Mum." She jumped back up to recover what was left of our vegetables for dinner, and my dad joined us conveniently as the serious conversation came to an end.

My dad was a large man, he liked to say it was because he was big boned and not at all because he snacked constantly throughout the day and all evening. I would never understand how my mum resisted his constant offers to share his food. He took a seat opposite me and commented on my cherry coloured skin. I assured him I wasn't burnt and it would fade into a lovely tan sooner or later.

They asked what I was planning to do the rest of the summer before I left for university, a conversation we'd had before. I explained to them again about how other than packing and buying things I might need I planned to not do anything except relax. It seemed as though they didn't completely agree with that plan, but they didn't push me.

I had worked after school and on weekends and school holidays for two years as a waitress at one of the small local cafes. When it closed down earlier that year after a particularly slow winter, I made the decision not to look into getting anything else. I'd saved a lot of my wages over the years and was quite happy to live on those for a while. I'd thought I would have a pretty carefree summer and get a job when things got serious again when I started university.

As an only child with two working parents, I had been left to my own devices a lot and had earned a fair bit of trust and respect from them. Occasionally, over the years, it had bothered me that they were both out so much, but when I really thought about it, I admired how hard they worked. I knew deep down that they would make time for me every second they were home if I asked them to.

Mum had started working part-time in a local café when she and my dad first moved there after I was born. She then worked her way up and became manager.

In the evening, after the café closed, it would reopen as a restaurant, with a different manager to run that side. It wasn't long before they started calling my mum into help as a waitress in the evenings as well. She told me she'd thought she had the ideal job; decent pay, daytime hours so she would be home in the morning and evening for her husband and daughter. But when she knows the restaurant is understaffed she can't say no to helping out.

Dad is an estate agent; he covers quite a wide radius so he's pretty busy as well. Luckily, it's a job that he doesn't bring home with him. My parents were opposites in that way. Often my mum would be thinking about staffing and ordering and getting stock ready for her next shift all through her evening off, while my dad stopped thinking of his job as soon as he arrived home.

My parents often worked opposite hours as they worked on a shift basis, and so I often found myself spending time with just one of them at a time. Perhaps that was why they were so affectionate with each other when they did get some time off at the same time.

It made sense that as their daughter I would want to work too. But as an eighteen-year-old about to go to university, I didn't want to waste my summer, and with Jeremy's arrival in my life, I couldn't imagine trying to manage having a job as well.

-

That night at the park, everything seemed clearer, as if I had memorised every path, every stall, every ride. When I closed my eyes, I could see it all as clear as day.

Jeremy had dragged me straight over to one of the games but I was more interested in getting some answers.

"Jeremy, why is it always the same people here every night?"

He barely looked my way as he replied. "Do we have to talk about that now?"

"Yes," I said, taken aback. Why did he always avoid these questions? "There's so much that I just don't understand about this place."

"Why do you want to know so much?" Jeremy finally turned to me. With the full attention of his beautiful gaze on me I almost forget what we were talking about.

"Because I like it here and I want to know more," I said, finally.

"You like it here?" Jeremy beamed.

"Of course, I do."

"Do you like it enough to stay?" Hope filled his eyes and he took hold of both of my hands.

Biting my lip, I tried to remember why it was I kept saying no. "I come back every evening."

He squeezed my hands tighter. "What's keeping you there? You said yourself you weren't sure about going to university, so why not just stay here?"

For a moment, I had forgotten about university, and all the decisions I had been struggling with. Being reminded of my life outside the park stung. I tried to pull my hands from Jeremy's but he was too strong.

"Why don't you meet me in town tomorrow? I can show you some of the places I love as well." I suggested. Perhaps that would give him a reason to leave the park, and maybe he would enjoy it and want to come with me to university. The accommodation was so small but I was sure we would make it work.

"I can't!" he almost growled at me. "I'm not leaving the park."

"Jeremy," I begged. "You're hurting me, let go."

Finally, I pulled my hands free of his grip; white splotches remained where his fingers had been. Something was changing in Jeremy; he didn't seem to be the same fun-loving boy I had met in the woods a few nights earlier.

Was it my fault? I wondered, helplessly.

The rest of the evening felt strained. Jeremy barely spoke to me and I found myself following him around, and cheering as he expertly played game after game, trying to feel close to him again.

I wanted to stay that night, as if staying at Jeremy's Amusement Park as he wanted would right my wrongs and he would no longer be angry with me. But Mrs. Millar's disapproving face appeared before me before I could let that idea fully form, shuffling me away from Jeremy's uninterested body and out of the park.

# Chapter 17

I couldn't rid my mind of Jeremy's angry face as I wandered into town that morning. My legs led me slower than normal and when I noticed the cafes were already open, I decided a coffee would help to clear the fog in my mind.

The young barista took my order at the counter and I waited for my takeaway americano with a splash of milk to be ready. My eyes travelled over the empty wooden tables in the café, the menus and sugars bowls all placed neatly in the centre of each one, the chairs tucked perfectly out of the way.

Only one customer inhabited any of the café tables. He sat at the back of the café, coffee in one hand and phone in the other.

My eyes lingered over him. He looked familiar to me in some way I couldn't quite put my finger on. His jawline was sharp and his nose had a bit of a point to it. His dark hair had been cut short and his t-shirt hung loosely over his body.

It wasn't until his breathtaking emerald eyes lifted to meet mine that I knew who he reminded me of. He looked like an older, slimmer, and more defined Jeremy. Although his eyes were a different colour they shared the same vibrancy.

Unlike Jeremy's pale moonlight skin, this man had a golden sun kissed tan.

He met me with a lopsided smile, forming a dimple on the right side and lifted his eyebrows ever so slightly.

"Miss," a voice said behind me. "Your coffee is ready."

Dragging my eyes back to the barista, I thanked her and picked up my takeaway coffee cup, before turning back to the mystery man.

I stepped cautiously towards where he was now looking back at his phone.

"Excuse me," I said, shyly. "I'm really sorry for staring, it's just that you look like someone I know."

"That's alright," he chuckled. His voice was a little deeper than Jeremy's. It occurred to me then, that if they were related in some way this might be my opportunity to find out more about Jeremy. He looked older than Jeremy, maybe twenty-one or twenty-two.

"Do you know someone called Jeremy? About my age."

His eyes seemed to harden and his eyes brows creased together. "Are you talking about Jeremy Brown?"

"I don't know his last name, actually. But he looks so similar to you."

The man looked a little uncomfortable before he offered for me to take the seat opposite him. I took him up on the offer, my eyes never leaving his face.

"How did you know him? You couldn't have been very old when it happened," the man asked.

"What do you mean? When what happened?"

The man's eyes searched mine for a few seconds, he looked as confused as I felt. "When he died."

Died? No, we couldn't be talking about the same person.

"My older brother Jeremy," the man continued. "He died ten years ago, at that amusement park. I get told all the time how a-like we look."

Ten years ago? No. A dark chill crept up my spine and it was all I could do to stop myself from shivering. Even as I told myself there could be no way he was dead, I had talked to him, felt his touch even, I still couldn't push away the horrible doubt building in my chest. Could that be why so many details about his life didn't make sense?

I took a deep breath, trying to compose myself as to not come off as mad as I felt.

"I'm so sorry."

"Thank you," the man said.

"Can I ask how he died?"

"It was on the roller coaster. There was a fault in the structure and it collapsed," the man explained. His thick eyebrows grew even closer together as he watched for my reaction. "You really didn't know?"

Stars took over my vision, and sweat began soak into my shirt as I stood up suddenly.

"I'm sorry. I have to go." I stumbled out of the café, ignoring the man's concerned voice calling after me.

I could barely look at any of the passersby as I practically ran all the way home. Sweat was building on my neck as the sun glared down upon me.

Everything made sense, why he couldn't leave the park, why he couldn't become a teacher, why he hadn't seen his family. It was because he had died ten years ago.

How had I seen him and talked to him and touched him? It didn't make any sense. Was I hallucinating? I must have hit my head somehow at the abandoned amusement park that night my friends and I had gone to investigate. That must have been what had happened. I would wake up soon laying on the ground and it would be only an hour after I passed out and my friends would be around me and they would be relieved to see me open my eyes. They would think my magical dreams were mad and they would laugh.

Wake up, I told myself desperately. Wake up! Wake up!

Sweat dripped from my face by the time I made it home.

Ignoring all the missed calls and messages on my phone I opened Google straight away and searched for Jeremy Brown.

A photo appeared immediately, staring at me from my phone screen. It was him. It was the smile I had begun to know so well and the eyes I could fall into. His hair was shorter there, as if freshly cut that day. It couldn't be him.

Same name, same eyes, same nose, same smile. Same person.

I read through the article so quickly the words began to blur and I had to slow myself down. The words "terrible accident" and "One dead at the scene and one in critical condition" stood out to me.

The image of Jeremy's lifeless body from my dream a few days ago flashed before my eyes. He'd been laying under the roller coaster. Maybe that was how he'd looked when he'd died ten years ago. What was I saying? He'd died? The thought of losing Jeremy now or ten years ago filled me with terror. Tears stung the back of my eyes as I imagined the pain he must have been in, the loss everyone around him must have felt losing him so suddenly.

As I continued to scan the news report, I found that it was his brother that had been sitting next to him and who had been left in critical condition. As he was a minor at the time, they hadn't given his name.

From what Jeremy had said about his brother it seemed like he meant everything to him, like he was his best friend and closest family. I couldn't imagine how his brother must have felt losing Jeremy.

The news report went on to say the accident was caused by a faulty mechanism that became weak and collapsed after too much use. The amusement park was closed down immediately, around fifty people lost their jobs, and the park was abandoned.

Staring at the ceiling with my head on my pillow and my duvet pulled high up to my neck, images of Jeremy flew through my mind. He had seemed so alive. Not only in the physical way, but in that he was so full of energy and playfulness.

What was I going to do?

# Chapter 18

Fuzziness kept a tight hold of my head when I woke up and I had to sit up slowly to stop myself getting dizzy. Soft puffy skin surrounded my eyes and my face felt warm to touch.

During the few hours I had slept, I'd dreamt about Jeremy's Amusement Park. That seemed to be all I could think about, while awake or asleep. I dreamt of the Jeremy I had met on the first night at the park, his immature smile, and how he had been so excited to show me his park. Dream Jeremy seemed to beckon me further in until I could no longer find the exit.

I didn't know why at the time, but confusion had laced every second of my dream. It was only when I woke up, I remembered the truth. That Jeremy was dead. I let my mind wonder what that could really mean.

Was he a spirit? A ghost? Or a mere figment of my imagination?

If he were some sort of spirit or ghost, why was he here? And why was I the only one that could see him?

I had to know more about him, to know what kind of a person he was before it happened. I took my phone from where it lay on my wooden bedside table and Googled him once again. More news reports came up, all giving the same information about the accident, it seemed no one in his family wanted to make a comment. Who could blame them? One report mentioned a lawsuit against the park, but nothing seemed to have come of that.

As I scrolled further down the Google search, I found a Facebook page belonging to Jeremy Brown. Why wouldn't he have social media accounts? It wasn't that long ago, I thought, kicking myself for not thinking of that sooner. I clicked on it and found first a photo of Jeremy that hadn't been used in any news reports. His profile picture was of him, dressed smartly in a shirt and trousers, his hair short and neat. It must have been from a wedding or prom or something similar.

Further down were birthday messages from old friends and family members sharing photos with him and describing the pain they felt without him. His birthday was on February 9th.

I looked further down the page and found messages people had left him. Lots of messages from people sending their condolences, telling him how much they would miss him. I wondered if Jeremy had any idea these messages were here.

There was a photo from what looked like a family event, Jeremy, his two parents and his younger brother. Even though the faces in the photo were small the similarities between each of them was obvious. Underneath was a photo of Jeremy with a group of guys all dressed in what appeared to be basketball uniforms. They weren't the sort of team you would see playing professionally, they ranged in shapes and sizes and Jeremy fit perfectly in the middle of the group. He was grinning wildly, they all were. I wondered if it had been a practice or a competition game when that photo was taken.

More photos were showing up, and in every one Jeremy had a large grin on his face, as if he was always enjoying life and nothing could get him down. I came across a photo of Jeremy next to a girl, she was pretty in a simple kind of way, no makeup or fancy dress, just her dark hair in plaits and a simple pink dress. Who was she? I wondered. A small part of me was jealous of her closeness to him, but I reminded myself that it didn't matter now, because they could never see each other again.

It was in that moment that it dawned on me; a romantic relationship with Jeremy would be impossible. A small feeling of betrayal nagged at my brain, why would Jeremy lead me on and let me get my hopes up if he knew we could never have anything together? Had he really expected me to never learn the truth?

I scrolled so far down that the condolence messages came to an end and there was a post that appeared to be made by Jeremy himself.

"Great game tonight! We're in the finals. Can't wait for next week's game!" There were a few photos of him and his team playing basketball, I assumed they had been taken that day. The knot at the back of my throat grew again, and tears stung my eyes, as I thought about how much he would have missed, how much he could have done.

I continued looking at his other posts, mostly it was just things other people had tagged him in, days out with his friends, nights on the town, family events and gatherings. It seemed like he got out a lot and had a large group of friends. Of course, he did, I thought to myself. Who could resist the positive energy that radiated from his whole being, like a mist of happy feelings? I was a willing victim, unable to stay away from him since the first night we'd met.

A thought occurred to me as I scrolled through his old social media: how lonely he must have been, stuck in that amusement park for so long. It was almost too sad to think about. Perhaps that was why he had brought me there, and why he wanted me to stay. I had no idea what it must be like to be a spirit stuck on earth after death in a sort of purgatory, could I really blame him for his mood swings?

Overcome with a sudden determination, I jumped out of bed and dressed quickly.

Downstairs, with some jam on toast and cup of coffee I opened my laptop and got to work.

First, I searched "Purgatory" and read the first description to appear.

"A place of suffering inhabited by the souls of sinners who are looking to make amends for their sins before moving on to heaven."

Could Jeremy have committed any sins? I wondered.

I was sure he couldn't have sinned enough to warrant a stay in purgatory. I was sure if Jeremy had committed a crime of any kind the reporters would have found about it and included it in the piece about his death.

I decided to move on from this idea and instead search "how do spirits get stuck on earth".

The first article I clicked on had a list of reasons for spirits to stay on earth.

"1. When a loved one cannot let go of their attachment to the deceased.

2. The deceased does not realise they have died.

3. When the deceased fears retribution for sins they have committed.

4. A curse or hex.

5. Having unfinished business."

I considered the first option, the only way I could find out if Jeremy's family were hanging on to their attachment to him was to meet them and talk to them. Even with the quick interaction with his younger brother at the café that morning, I didn't know how I would go about talking to them. I put that idea to the back of my mind to revisit after looking into other options.

I hadn't considered the second option. What if he didn't even know he was dead? I made a mental note to find out as soon as I got the park that evening.

Option three was possible, but again it made me wonder what exactly he could need retribution for. What sins could Jeremy have committed? This option would at least explain why he didn't seem interested in passing on.

I didn't believe in magic, so option four was a no. Although, I hadn't believed in seeing and hanging out with spirits so I supposed I couldn't completely rule it out.

Which brought me to number five. Unfinished business. This one sounded the most likely to me, and would be the first thing I would discuss with Jeremy.

For now, I decided to look at his family, specifically his brother. Through a little more sleuthing I found out that his brother's name was Liam.

I searched his name and found more than one Facebook account belonging to Liam Brown, after looking through a few accounts with photos of middle-aged men and one teenager I finally found it. His profile picture popped up and there he was. Even in a photo I could see the similarities he shared with Jeremy.

The photo was a little blurred and hard to figure out but his features stood out to me. His nose was just the same as Jeremy's but his chin and cheek bones were a little sharper. It was his eyes that stuck out to me, just as they had in the café. I wondered for a minute if they each took after a different parent, and which parent it was they received their eye colour from.

I scrolled down his profile to find that he had only posted a handful of times. He must have been quite a private person. It was clear that he hadn't had any social media before the accident. Going by the age on his profile, twenty-two, he would have only been twelve when the accident happened.

It looked as though he was tagged in more posts and photos then he uploaded himself and he appeared to be just as popular as his older brother had been.

His profile gave away no extra details of the accident, and with the little he posted I couldn't tell what he was doing with his life now.

The only thing I could think to do next was to send him a message. I appologised for my abrupt exit earlier and told him that I had known Jeremy. As I would have been eight at the time, I couldn't say I was his friend, so I had to think of something else. Seeing as Jeremy seemed to be a pretty decent person, I said that I'd known him when he had volunteered to teach basketball to kids. I finished the message by asked to see Liam again. After that, I had to wait.

My mum wandered through the front door of the house, her sun kissed shoulders bare under her strappy vest, and made her way into the living room.

"Mae," she said in surprise.

"Hi, Mum." I smiled at her. She took the bag she was carrying into the kitchen and I heard her unpacking things into cupboards.

Somehow, I found my way back to Jeremy's profile and looked again through photos of him, photos of when he was alive.

"What are you doing home?" Mum asked, passing me a glass of lemonade with ice cubes floating on the surface. She sat next to me with her own drink. "Who's that?"

Closing the lid of my laptop quickly and putting it on the table in front of us I told her he was no one. How could I explain my sudden infatuation with some random guy who'd died ten years ago?

"Mum?" I said curiously. "What do you think happens when you die?"

She lifted her thin eyebrows and sat straighter in her seat. "Well," she began. "That's a tough question. I like to think that there's a heaven of some form."

"You don't think spirits can stay on Earth after the person dies? Like if they're stuck somehow."

"I suppose they could get stuck here, but there's usually a reason for it which they can resolve and then move on."

I nodded thoughtfully, glad to have an opinion from a real person and not just articles from spiritual people online.

"Why are you asking?"

"I don't know," I said. "Just something someone said I guess."

# Chapter 19

Liam replied within the hour and suggested we meet for a coffee. He was free that afternoon and I scrambled to agree and quickly got myself ready.

Nerves were setting in as I wondered if I should tell him the truth, about how I had been visiting his dead brother recently.

We met in the same café as I had seen him in that morning, which was on the far side of town and by the time I arrived my face was red and sweat dripped down my back. I spent a couple of minutes preparing myself outside, straightening my summer blouse and flattening the frizz in my hair.

I spotted him instantly as I stepped through the door. Even from across the room I was taken aback by just how much he looked like Jeremy. I took a deep breath and dodged through the busy tables until I came to his.

"Liam," I greeted him shyly. He looked up suddenly, clearly surprised at my presence.

"Hi, sorry, I was completely in my own world there," he said, standing up and reaching out his hand for mine. I shook it, feeling his warmth spread over my skin. His eyes took my breath away. Gorgeous and vibrant even out of the day light.

We sat opposite each other, and I allowed my eyes to once again search his face. I noticed an air of maturity surrounding him comfortably.

"How are you?" I asked him.

"I'm a little nervous," he admitted. "It's been a while since anyone's wanted to talk about him."

I nodded in agreement. "I'm sorry if this is too painful for you, I can go."

"No," he laughed. It lacked the immaturity of Jeremy's laugh but the sound was so similar. "It's nice to remember him with someone else who knew him. I didn't know he taught basketball to kids. Did you know him well?"

It was a difficult question; I couldn't tell him how I hadn't known Jeremy while he was alive and I had only started to know him recently. I decided to answer as truthfully as I could and just leave out some of the more unbelievable details.

"Yes, quite well. He was such a great person." As I said it I realised I really had no idea what kind of person he was outside of playing games and eating sweets.

"He had his moments." Liam didn't look sad, he looked more content with the nice memory of his brother.

I decided to find out if the amusement park was really that significant to Jeremy. Why was he trapped there if it wasn't?

"He used to talk about an amusement park a lot. Did he always love going?"

Liam winced ever so slightly and I realised how insensitive it was for me to bring up the place his brother had died. Although I felt like I needed answers, I was sure Liam didn't want reminding of it.

"Not as far as I know. We only went together to get away from our parent's arguing." I was surprised to hear this little detail. We hadn't talked much about Jeremy's family but he had always made it seem like they were an average happy family.

Liam pulled a face. "They hadn't been getting on for a while, but when my mum filed for divorce it got a lot worse. With neither of them actually moving out of the house it became a pretty difficult place to be."

"I'm so sorry to hear that. I had no idea," I told him.

"Jeremy didn't like to admit the truth about how bad it was so instead he would ignore it by just going out. He never was one for serious situations, although he liked to be the cause of them sometimes. It often felt as if he was living in his own delirious world where nothing was ever wrong."

"He definitely has a way of changing the subject when you have something serious to say," I admitted, and then when I caught sight of Liam's quizzical face, I corrected myself. "Had. I meant had."

We sipped our coffees for a few moments and thought about Jeremy. Liam didn't seem to be crippled or mentally affected by the accident, but I needed to know for sure.

"Do you mind if I ask, how did you… How did you survive the accident?"

Liam didn't look offended by my question.

"Really good doctors," he laughed. "I was in a really bad way, and it took a long time to recover. I was in hospital for a few weeks and then I went through years of physio before I could walk fully. But eventually things got back into place and my body is pretty much back to normal."

"I'm glad you recovered," I said. "What do you do now? Are you working?"

"Not at the moment. I'm only here for the summer, I have a job near my university."

I was glad to hear it. That meant that at the very least Jeremy's death didn't send Liam into any sort of downward spiral, or if it had he had hit rock bottom a long time ago and was working for his future now.

"What course are you taking?"

"I'm training to be a vet."

"That's great," I told him. "Did you always want to be a vet?"

"Not always," Liam admitted thoughtfully. "Jeremy died just before he should have been going to university, so when it came to the time I should be applying I couldn't focus my mind on anything other than that fact. So, I took a year off, and in that time I started working at an animal rescue centre. I realised that I love animals and after a bit of research I decided a vet would the best choice."

Maybe that meant something good actually came from the horrible event; somehow it led to Liam finding something he enjoyed and something he could work towards.

"It's ironic, actually," Liam continued. "My parents had been furious when Jeremy told them he was no longer planning to go to university.

But when I told them my plans they didn't object or even really seem surprised."

I asked Liam a little more about his courses and his experiences and university, telling him I was about to start my first year and I was a little nervous.

He told me how he had kept himself a little shut away to begin with, focusing on his long-term goal instead of making friends or socialising. He smiled. "But then I came home over the Christmas holidays, and hung out with an old friend, and it felt so good, and so natural, and I realized I didn't want to be alone anymore. When I got back for the next term, I really put myself out there, started joining my housemates when they went out, you know. Sometimes you forget that you need more than just one big goal in life," Liam said. "You need to have fun occasionally as well."

He was right, of course. It was easy to forget such things as fun and friends. It felt as though I'd had more fun with Jeremy the last few days than I'd had in months, maybe years. I'd spent so long working towards exams so I could go to university that it made it difficult to relax. Breaking up with George had made concentrating on my exams a lot harder, which had made me more determined to do it.

I remembered when Jayne had told me how boring I had been recently that first night that we went to the abandoned amusement park, and I knew she was right. Even when I'd accepted their invitations to things, I still didn't really try to have any fun, I just assumed I wouldn't and so I didn't.

"What are you planning to do at university?" Liam asked, interrupting my deep thoughts. I told him about my ambitions and why I'd chosen accounting.

Liam's story was sadly inspiring to me, and I found myself hoping that he succeeded and he continued to find things that made him happy and that kept him going. I wondered how Liam's life would have gone if Jeremy hadn't died. Would he still have found his way to university, doing the same training he was doing now? I squashed the thought away before I could allow it to fill me with never ending what-ifs.

Curious to know more about the two brothers' home life I persevered on my quest for answers.

"So, which parent do you get your eyes from?" Every time I looked at Liam while we talked or I felt his eyes on me I felt drawn to the vibrant colour.

Liam laughed at my question. "I get mine from our mum and Jeremy's were our dad's."

"Do you get asked that a lot?" I asked awkwardly.

"Quite a lot," he said, not unhappily.

"They do stand out." I looked at my hands, suddenly embarrassed.

-

"It was nice to talk to you today, Mae," Liam said as we finished our coffee and made our way out of the cafe. Somehow, we had steered off the subject of Jeremy a while ago and I had found myself getting to know a lot about Liam and he had asked a lot about me too.

He liked thrillers and war films, he was moving out of university accommodation and into a flat with two other guys after the summer, he didn't like cooking so ate mostly microwave meals, and his favourite dog breed was a German Shepherd.

I also noticed how the veins were clear to see on his hands, and his nails looked short from biting. His hair was short but it still moved as he did, as if he had no gel or hair products in. His smooth face was cleanly shaven and his voice was ever so slightly deeper than Jeremy's.

"Thank you for meeting with me," I said.

Walking home my head filtered through everything we had talked about. Was it bad to find inspiration from someone else's tragedy? Knowing how quickly everything could change, how quickly everything could end was filling me with doubts.

One of life's biggest questions floated through my mind. "If I died now, would I be happy with the life I've had?"

I wasn't sure I could answer that question.

Muggy summer heat wrapped around my skin and I felt a storm brewing far away, I was sure it would hit us in a day or two. I wondered if I could go to Jeremy's Amusement Park if it was stormy. Would the storm make it to the park or did it have its own weather system?

I considered calling Jayne to make the most of my time while I could, have some fun with my friends before we all moved to different places and all they remembered me as was boring. Exhaustion filled my chest before I could take my phone out and contact any of my friends. All of these all-night excursions were starting to get to me. I needed to get some sleep.

Rest didn't seem to find me well during daylight hours. Sleeping with the sun shining through the cracks in my curtains was preventing me from finding the deep sleep my body required.

Pulling the duvet over my head I groaned as my thoughts kept me awake. It was only a few hours until I needed to wake up and make my way back to Jeremy's Amusement Park; it was beginning to feel just as much a part of my routine as eating dinner or brushing my teeth.

Sleep finally came and I fell into dreams of uncertainty and confusion. More often than not nowadays my dreams seemed to lead me to more questions than my waking brain could think of, all of which disappeared when consciousness regained hold of me.

In my mind I went over everything I had found out through Google and talking to Liam, ready to confront Jeremy

Even at midnight outside in the midst of the dark forest sweat dripped down my back, the warmth tight around my limbs. Branches encroached on the pathway I had formed between the thick trees where only I walked. I half-heartedly pushed them out of my way and forced my legs forwards.

It was occurring to me that Jeremy might not like my new found knowledge of his situation. What if he stopped me coming back now that I knew the truth? The sooner I got there, the sooner I would have to tell him what I knew.

What if I don't tell him? I thought. I could just continue visiting the park, as I have been, and now I know the truth I won't have to keep pushing him and he won't get so angry.

No. I shook my head. I still had so many questions, I had to confront Jeremy.

He was waiting at the entrance of the park, just as he was every night, and I smiled sadly at him.

"Are you okay?" he asked, taking my hand.

"I need to talk to you about something," I admitted, taking in his caring eyes. "We should probably talk in private."

He turned from me and began walking away from the crowds of people watching us. He stopped when we came to a teepee shaped tent, this one was a midnight blue colour. No fairy lights lined the outside of this tent, making it almost impossible to see from afar.

Jeremy held open the curtain door for me to slide inside. Furry rugs covered the floor with plump silk pillows surrounding the only light source in the tent: an intricately detailed lamp, that perched on a small table in the centre of the tent with a flickering candle inside.

I sat on the far side of the tent feeling nervous all of a sudden. Jeremy sat a few feet away from me, the skin on his sharp face was golden from the lamp's glow. Neither of us spoke for a long time.

"You're dead," I said finally.

He didn't even look surprised.

"You knew then?" I asked.

"I had a feeling, but I didn't know for sure," he admitted.

"Why are you still here? Why haven't you moved on or something?"

"I have no idea," Jeremy confessed. "I remember the accident. I can still feel it. After it happened, I blacked out and woke up here."

I pondered on his answer long enough for Jeremy to ask me a question. "Do you know... Do you know how long ago it happened?"

"About ten years ago," I told him gently.

Jeremy looked me in the eyes, panic clearly filling him. "That long?"

I nodded.

Silence filled the tent again and I hugged my knees to my chest as I watched the flame flickering inside the lamp. I felt as though Jeremy was somewhere else entirely now, he could neither see me nor hear me while he tortured himself with all the things he didn't know.

"What about my brother, Liam?" Panic suddenly took over Jeremy. "He was on the ride with me. I need to know if he is alright."

"He's fine," I assured him.

"How do you know?"

"I ran into him in town," I confessed. "He looks just like you."

Jeremy appeared to calm down. "You're sure he's okay?"

"Yes, I talked to him. He's fine. He was in hospital for a while but he recovered."

Once again, Jeremy remained silent, and I was tempted to leave him that way, but I had more questions to be answered and he was the only one who could do so.

"Can anyone else see you? Has anyone else been here?"

Jeremy slowly arose from his dark thoughts and re-entered my line of questioning. "I don't know. I've only tried once and that was with you."

"You said you couldn't leave and yet you left to bring me here."

"I can go as far as the forest line. When I got to the forest entrance, I saw you sat on the other side."

"But on that first night we walked through the forest for quite a while to get here."

Jeremy looked uncertain for a moment. "For me, I took your hand and pulled you straight through. There was no long walk."

"Well... When I came during the day that didn't work. I couldn't find the park at all."

"That's because it's always night here. The sun begins to rise and then it sets again."

"Why?" There were so many things that were still not making sense, my list of questions was just getting longer.

"How should I know?"

"Well, it's your park."

"Mae," Jeremy said, looking sympathetically at me, and giving me a chance to soak up the beautiful blue of his eyes again. "Look, one day I just woke up here. No one was waiting for me to explain why or how it all works. Since then, it's been up to me to get to know this park. I'd always assumed that after death there's nothing, or maybe there was a heaven or something else."

"This isn't heaven for you?"

"Don't get me wrong, I loved visiting the amusement park when I was alive. And as much as I've enjoyed my time here, this isn't what I imagined heaven to be."

"Then why are you here?" I wondered aloud.

# Chapter 20

Jeremy seemed to be in a positive mood after discussing the truth. We were still without answers but for now at least Jeremy had me, even if he was stuck spending every day in an amusement park that seemed to be put there especially for him.

He slowly scooched closer to me on the comfy pillows and was soon sitting close enough for me to feel the warmth radiating from his body. He nudged me with his shoulder and smiled encouragingly.

When I'd first arrived at Jeremy's Amusement Park it had seemed as though it was his favourite place in the world and I was honoured to be chosen to see it. But now I wondered if it wasn't more that he was just excited not to be by himself any more, to share his new home with someone else.

"Do you sleep?" I asked, suddenly curious if he did in fact have a home here.

"No," he said. "Sometimes I come here just to rest from the madness outside. But I haven't slept the whole time I've been here. No one has." Why would he need to dream when he had no future? A bitter voice from inside me said.

The silence around us seemed almost sad. I felt as though I could just about forget that Jeremy was dead, and just be happy to spend time with him while he was still there, but then I thought of how I could never see him in the daylight, could never take him to my house, or go on a date that was somewhere that wasn't the amusement park. What would happen when I got older and he didn't?

The thought of growing older and moving on with my life while Jeremy remained stuck at eighteen sent dread through my body. I couldn't leave him behind.

I remembered, suddenly, something he had said earlier. "You said you're stuck here?"

"That's right. I've tried to leave but it's like there is an invisible wall where the forest begins."

"Well, maybe you are stuck," I said, not entirely sure where I was going with this. "So, maybe, we just need to unstick you somehow."

"Unstick me?" Jeremy laughed.

"I mean, there's got to be a reason you're here and not in heaven or wherever people normally go."

"Okay." He nodded thoughtfully. "What's keeping me here?"

"How am I supposed to know?" We both sighed again, another wall standing in our way.

After a moment Jeremy looked at me seriously. "Do you want me to leave then? You don't want to keep seeing me?"

I took his hand in mine. "Of course not! I want to be with you all the time. But that's part of the problem. We can only see each other at night."

Jeremy didn't seem to understand why this was a problem.

"I'll be going to university soon and I'll only be back for a little while over the holidays, are you just going to wait around for me?"

"Well, I don't have much else to do."

"And what about when I'm fifty and you're still eighteen?"

His eyebrows creased and a small groan poured from his throat. "I don't know. Can't we just talk about that when it comes to it?"

"This is what I'm talking about Jeremy." I tried to keep my voice light, tried to make him understand that this wasn't normal. "We can't wait until I'm fifty. I can't spend the next thirty-two years pining for a boy I can never really be with."

"You'd pine over me?" Jeremy smirked, easing the tension between us.

"I can't live my life here," I said, unable to look Jeremy in his hopeful eyes. He wrapped his arm around me and pulled me to his chest.

"Well, why can't you live here?"

I pulled away from him again to see in his face if he was joking. It appeared he was not.

"My life is out there, Jeremy. I can't just leave all my friends and family, and live here for eternity."

"It's nice here, Mae, you'll enjoy it." The idea seemed to be forming rapidly in his mind and he smiled with excitement. "You can share this tent with me, or you can have a private tent. And we can just hang out and go on rides."

I took a deep breath, approaching the next subject softly. "Jeremy, how about we figure out why you're stuck here? That way maybe you could move on to heaven. Heaven will be much nicer than this place."

I wondered desperately if he genuinely thought I could stay with him or just continue visiting him every night. As much as I hated to admit it, I didn't think I could keep up these visits for much longer. I missed the daytime sun, I missed feeling awake, and I missed my old life. Maybe I was being selfish but I couldn't let him stay.

Jeremy looked down at his lap, contemplating what to say to me. "Mae, how do you know where I'll go?" he said nervously. "What if I go somewhere worse?"

"Why would you?" I asked him, confused by his sudden change of heart. "You're a good person, Jeremy."

Suddenly a smile grew on his face and I saw the energy coming back to him. "How about we talk about that later? Seeing as you're here, let's do something fun together."

Something felt wrong, Jeremy clearly wasn't keen on the idea of moving on, but I thought he would agree with me in the end. Against my better judgement I agreed to spend some more time with him until later in the night when I would bring it up to him again.

Jeremy took my hand and pulled me out of the teepee. A chill crept up my arm from where he touched me and I almost jerked my arm away. He was normally so warm; I couldn't understand what was happening. "Where are we going?" I asked nervously.

"It's a surprise, something I haven't shown you yet," Jeremy said, without looking at me.

He led me further away from the flashing lights and noisy games. My eyes searched the shadows as the light seemed to fade away behind us, and all the tents, now dark and velvety, appeared to be private and not meant for guests of the park.

The beating in my chest began to speed up when I tried to pull my hand free of Jeremy's tight grip.

"We're almost there," he said mysteriously.

Soon it was so dark I could barely see where he was leading me, the sounds from the park were so faint behind us I wondered if anyone would even know we were there. I hadn't known the park went that far. Maybe this area was where all the workers lived, I thought to myself. Would they need somewhere to live if they were just figments of Jeremy's imagination?

Jeremy opened what sounded like a metal door and let me go ahead of him, releasing my hand only when I was inside. With a loud bang he slammed the door shut behind me and it was only then I realised I was in a large metal cage. I swung around to look at Jeremy, backing away from me.

"Jeremy!" I shouted, panic making my voice harsh.

"I'm sorry, Mae," he said. "I had no other choice; I can't let you leave!" The Jeremy I thought I knew was gone, replaced with someone sinister. He turned his back to me and ran towards the bright lights of the park. His figure soon disappeared.

My eyes remained desperately searching the distant lights and the ant-like families I could just about make out. I could barely fathom the reality of what had just happened, how it had happened. The icy feeling of the metal on my hands brought a shock through my system and I sat back suddenly.

Adapting quickly to the lack of light my eyes searched the darkness around me. The cage was larger than I expected, allowing me to stand tall without hitting my head and it was the same distance wide. A very serious question formed in my head, why was there a human sized cage in Jeremy's Amusement Park?

Robbed of all energy, I slid to the ground, which I was surprised to find was made of cold stone, and let the air in my chest out in one long breath.

I sat for a long time, all thoughts and hope lost. Soon I found my legs had curled up to my chest and I wrapped my arms around them helplessly.

Images of Jeremy's friendly face and welcoming smile seeped into my mind as I wondered how he could do this to me. Was the childlike innocence he portrayed all just an act?

I remembered all the conversations we'd had, all the times he had made me laugh, but more than that I remembered all the times he had spoken and led me to more unanswered questions. I remembered how unenthusiastic he'd seemed when I had suggested finding a way for him to move on.

A shadow of light flickered and tricked me into thinking Jeremy's figure was returning to me. When my heart returned to its normal rhythm, I realised I couldn't just wait for his return, I had to do something.

"Help!" I shouted as loud as I could force my voice to go. "Help!"

I screamed and shouted until my throat felt raw and my voice refused to carry on, falling once again to the cold, hard ground, defeated by the emptiness surrounding my cries.

A violet hue began to take over the night sky as the mysterious sun rose slowly.

Things became clearer in the early morning light, and I spotted a row of deep velvet tents, with lanterns hanging around the doorways but with no candles lit inside.

As the night came to an end, I noticed not a soul had entered any one of the tents around me and I wondered if any of the others contained cages just like mine. With the curtain doors closed there was no way for me to know what lay inside.

The path Jeremy had led me on to reach the cage where he abandoned me was overgrown and covered in patches of grass and weeds. The brilliant colour of the tents surrounding now seemed to be faded and dirty, the bottom rims were ratty and some of the doorway ways appeared almost on an angle as if collapsed over time.

Just as quickly as the sun had appeared the sky began to darken again just like Jeremy had said it would when he told me there was no day time in the amusement park. Did that mean I had lost an entire day in the real world?

Sleep didn't come for me that night, my body was pulsing with the energy from Jeremy's betrayal, and furious questions took over my mind. I had no idea how much time passed that second night, nothing seemed to move around me, the noises from the park remained distant and the lights barely made it to me.

Finally, while leaning against the back of the cage opposite the door I noticed a figure growing closer. As the figure came to the door of the cage, I realised it was Jeremy, he had a striped pink and brown paper bag in his hand, his guilty eyes remained glued to the ground as he drew closer to me as if he didn't want to look at me at all. I kept quiet, waiting to see what he said or if he let me out.

"I brought you something to eat," Jeremy said softly, squeezing the paper bag through one of the gaps between the bars and letting it fall into the cage.

"I'm not hungry," I told him honestly.

He shrugged his shoulders, keeping his eyes low and away from my own. "Doesn't really matter, no one really needs to eat here."

"Aren't I the first person you've brought here? How would you know if I need to eat or not?"

"I'm just guessing," Jeremy admitted.

"What am I doing here, Jeremy?" I said, suddenly furious with him.

"I can't move on, Mae. I want to stay here. With you."

"You're just scared," I said.

"No!" Jeremy shouted, suddenly looking in my eyes. I was shocked at how wildly bright his own were even in this dark area of the park. "What does it matter anyway? No one will ever find this place again and I can just stay here forever."

"Why don't you let me go then? I could go back to my own life and never mention you to anyone." I stood up on my aching legs but remained firmly against the back wall.

"You'll tell someone! I can't let you do that."

"You're dead, Jeremy. You're a spirit stuck on earth; don't you think you should move on to heaven?"

"I wasn't a good person, Mae!" Jeremy shouted suddenly, and then his broad shoulders sunk in defeat and he spoke quietly after that. "I don't know if I will go to heaven because I wasn't a good person before I died."

The surprise must have been written all over my face as Jeremy took a deep breath and continued.

"I wasn't a good brother; I was barely talking to Liam by that time. I guess we naturally grew apart when I was a teenager but I deliberately kept it that way when I knew Liam wanted to be close again. The only reason we were together the night of the accident was because our parents kicked us both out of the house while they were fighting and none of my friends were around. It was my fault my parents were even fighting in the first place; it was usually my fault. I was always telling them things that would upset them. They knew me so well at the park because I used to skip lessons with my friends and we would go there for hours most days, just messing around and causing trouble mostly. I knew Liam didn't have that many friends and I would just leave him to deal with our parents constantly raging at each other and us when we were home."

"None of what you just said is that bad," I told him.

"I'm not leaving," he said.

I took a deep breath, I was getting nowhere with Jeremy on the matter. "Why have you even got a cage here?" I asked bitterly.

"I found it a while ago, I think I remember hearing before the accident the park was looking into having live animals for shows. Sort of like a circus, I guess."

"And you just happened to have the key?" I asked.

"It was left in the door when I found it." What Jeremy was saying sounded logical, but I noticed he still wasn't opening the door and releasing me from his amusement park.

"Why did you bring me here in the first place?"

"You looked sad, I thought you could do with having some fun. And... I guess I wanted some company." Jeremy didn't appear to feel any guilt over his actions.

"So, you were never really drawn to me, it could have been any sad person sitting there and you would have brought them to the park."

"Well... I guess... It's not how it sounds. I just wanted someone to share this place with." I was realising that Jeremy had never really cared about me in the way I had cared for him.

"Let me out of here, Jeremy," I demanded.

"Look, just think about it, okay? I think you would really like it here if you stopped resisting," he said as he turned his back to me. "I'll come back later or tomorrow."

I shot forward to the front of the cage and slipped my arm through to grip his shirt tightly. "You're leaving me here again?"

Jeremy pulled his shirt free of my grip and carried on walking forward.

In a last attempt to save myself I shouted the only thing I could think of. "I told my friends about this place! They'll come looking for me, they'll see through your illusion."

"No one can see you while you are here. You're as invisible as I am." With that Jeremy disappeared back to the park lights.

Panic took over my body, coursing through my veins as sweat formed on the back of my neck. Picturing my parents, I wondered how they would feel when I never came home, I saw the fright on their faces, the police at our door, asking questions in order to figure out where I had gone. No one will find me here, I thought to myself.

For the first time since meeting Jeremy, I regretted every decision I had made leading to that point. I regretted going to the abandoned amusement park in the first place. I should have said no to my friends, I should have pushed to stay at the pub. I should never have returned to the park after finding out that Jeremy was dead.

A tight knot formed in my throat and tears fought to get free as I felt a wet burning sensation slide over my cheeks. I allowed the tears to soak into the top of my shirt as they swam over my face and down my neck. As much as I refused it access, a whimper forcefully escaped my lips and I gave in and allowed the sadness to take over me, crying and screaming until all the energy had gone from my defeated body and I sank into an overwhelming sleep.

-

"Wake up," a strong hand pushed my lifeless body. "Wake up you silly girl!"

I allowed my eyes to slowly open and adjust to the little light that made it into my cage. In front of me Mrs. Millar was crouched on her large knees, her face filled with concern as she stared at mine.

With a gasp I threw myself up and backed as far from her as I could. What was Jeremy up to now? I wondered to myself.

"What are you doing here?" I spat at her angrily.

"I'm here to get you out." She stuck out her hand and took hold of my wrist. "Come with me."

"Why should I?"

"Don't be a stupid girl, I'm trying to help you!" Fury filled Mrs. Millar's round face. "I never wanted you here in the first place, I'm not going to want you here forever."

I considered my options quickly and the only one that would get me out of the cage was if I followed Mrs. Millar and took my chances that she wasn't leading me into another trap.

Ripping my arm from her grip I agreed to follow her, keeping my eyes firmly set on her round back as she led me into the shadows behind the aged tents. We kept low and out of any spots of light, straying from the path as often as we could.

Mrs. Millar moved smoothly, as if this was not her first time sneaking around in the shadows.

It occurred to me that this might be my only hope at getting any real answers.

"Why was there a cage here?" I whispered urgently at Mrs. Miller's back.

She remained quiet as we grew closer to the bright lights of the amusement park and the screams of joy and laughter became clear again.

"Mrs. Millar, please!"

"Okay," she said, pulling me down into a crouch behind a tent that was significantly cleaner and better kept than the ones that had surrounded the cage. "He made it. He made it for you."

"He said it was already here, he said he found it a few days ago."

"If he found it it's because he wanted to. This is Jeremy's world; everything here was made by him. It's all a piece of work coming straight from his own mind."     A horrible thought struck me. "That means he made you too."

She gripped my arm tighter to stop me from backing away. "Keep your voice down," she warned. "He created me, yes. But I act as his conscience. When he makes decisions, I am there to tell him if they are bad. I told him it was a bad idea to bring you here in the first place, I told him not trap you. But he didn't listen to me. And now I am cleaning up his mess."

All the information I was now learning about Jeremy and about the park was swarming through my mind, pushing me from one way to another. I didn't know what to think. And above it all, there was the instinct for survival: I had to get out of there.

"How do I get out?" I asked decisively.

"Follow me," Mrs. Millar said, letting go of my wrist.

We weaved in and out of tent pegs until we were behind the first game stand in the amusement park. I peeked my head ever so slightly round the corner to see the same families and friends wandering past. Quickly, I sat back as a group of friends headed straight for the stand we hid behind.

A memory of me and Jeremy sitting between two stands came to mind. It was the evening we had talked and talked and I had felt as though I was getting to know him more that evening. I wondered if he had meant any of what he had said.

With a quick look around, Mrs. Millar was off again, making her way swiftly from stand to stand, avoiding the gaps between where people would be able to see us.

Adrenaline fueled me as I saw the exit ahead, there was one stand left and then all I would have to do would be to sprint across the open space to the end, pass the woman at the ticket table and through the trees.

Just as I could feel the freedom taking over me, my foot hooked onto a stone and my whole world went sideways as I fell heavily to the ground. A yelp escaped my lips before I could stop it.

Mrs. Millar turned back quickly and grabbed my waist, lifting me swiftly back into a standing position.

"Hurry now," she said.

A deep breath filled my lungs as I prepared to make a run for the exit and escape the unnatural hold Jeremy had on me.

"Mae!" It was him, calling from somewhere in the distance. I knew I shouldn't hesitate; I should go now before he could catch up with me, but some part of me wanted to see him again. I wanted to see my captor for the man he really was.

His eyes met mine from across the park, he was about the same distance from the exit as I was but on the opposite side. A kind smile was on his lips and he beckoned for me to come to him. Some part of me was tempted, I even turned my body in his direction. Was it the alluring blue of his eyes that almost convinced me to go back to him?

"Go, now!" Mrs. Millar's big hands shoved me toward the exit and I knew what I had to do. Taking off at a run I kept my head straight and ignored Jeremy calling my name. I could hear him growing closer but I refused to let my legs falter as I bolted out of the amusement park and through the tree line, almost toppling right over the fallen wall in the abandoned amusement park.

# Chapter 21

Hunger took a tight hold of my body as I escaped the realm of Jeremy's Amusement Park and I fell to my knees. It seemed that although I didn't require food while at the park my body hadn't forgotten that I'd gone without now that I was back in the real world.

Fighting the weakness in my knees I pushed myself up off the damp ground and forced myself to move across the abandoned amusement park until I reached the path on the other side.

With the last remaining bit of energy, I forced my legs to move faster and faster until I was running at full speed through the trees, ignoring the branches whipping at my face and the roots grabbing for my feet.

The sky was once again turning a deep violet colour as the sun began to wake up in the real world. When I emerged from the woodland and made my way back into town, I noticed the lack of any other life form, as my heavy footsteps echoed far into the distance. A couple of time I thought I heard Jeremy whispering my name, but every time I looked in the direction of his voice there was no one there.

My legs began to tire as I dragged them along the deserted streets, through the town and back home.

As I was closing the door quietly behind me and preparing to sneak up the stairs to change into a clean set of clothes before pretending I was just coming down for an early breakfast I heard footsteps emerging in the hallway at the top of the stairs.

"Mae!" my mum called down frantically. "Where have you been?" Panic filled her eyes as she flung her dressing gown around herself and ran down the stairs toward me.

Her arms were around my body before I could fully fathom what was happening, squeezing me tightly against her warmth.

My mind worked in overdrive as I tried desperately to come up with an excuse of why I might have been out for two days without even texting my parents to let them know I wouldn't be returning home. I couldn't tell my mum about Jeremy and his amusement park; she would think I was crazy. "I... I was at a friend's," I stuttered.

"Mae," she said seriously, holding me at arm's length to look me in the eyes as she spoke. "I know I've allowed you to go out at all hours of the night, returning home to sleep the day away. Maybe I should have been stricter about that. I thought I should respect your independence now, with university around the corner. But two days is too long to be gone without a word to either of us. We've been frantic."

"Mum, I'm sorry," I said helplessly.

"Where were you? Are you okay?" Mum asked and without giving me a chance to reply she continued while she dragged me by the arm and sat me next to her on the sofa. "I called Jayne, and she asked all your other friends and no one knew where you were. I was this close to calling the police."

I was embarrassed to think what my friend must be thinking, having my mum call them looking for me when I had barely talked to them at all that week.

An excuse suddenly came to my head. "Look I'm sorry, I've been seeing this new guy and I just got carried away." I knew spending two straight days with a new man wasn't the best way to calm my mum's nerves but what else could I say?

"A guy?" My mum's face fell in confusion and then quickly twisted in disgust. "You're going to throw your life away for a guy?"

I rolled my eyes. "I'm not throwing my life away."

"Mae! You cannot come home at five thirty in the morning after being out for two nights and then tell me this "guy" isn't convincing you to throw your life away. This is not like you. You are not an irresponsible person." She jumped up from her seat and began pacing the length of the living room, throwing her arms in the air as she spoke. Little did she know, she was actually right. Jeremy had actually asked me to throw my life away and stay with him at the park.

"You're living in my house, and as much as I don't want to pull this card, Mae, you've brought me to this." My mum sat down again as she started her speech, looking me seriously in the eyes. "You will follow my rules. You will be home by ten pm and you will not leave in the morning until you have seen either me or your dad and you will tell us where you will be and when you plan to be home. If anything changes you will call us to let us know. You will be home for dinner every night at six."

I opened my mouth to argue, but with my head fuzzy and my hunger clawing at my stomach I chose the option that would hopefully bring the conversation to an end the fastest. With a deep breath I agreed to her terms.

"Right," Mum said, seemingly not quite satisfied. "Now, seeing as we're up would you like some breakfast?"

"Let me get it, Mum," I said, patting her hand and getting slowly to my feet. It was the least I could do after what I had put them through.

I impatiently buttered a piece of bread and ate it while another two pieces each cooked in the toaster. I made myself and my mum a well needed coffee and slathered our toast in raspberry jam. We ate in silence and I relished the deliciousof the first food I had eaten in almost two days.

"I don't like you seeing this person," Mum finally said, after taking a long sip of her coffee.

"You don't even know him," I said, my teenage rebellion kicking in before I remembered that he had just captured me in a cage.

"Alright, Mae. I want to meet him. We'll have dinner with him this week. Invite him over. Then I can decide for myself."

"I really don't think that's necessary," I said, backtracking. "I don't think it is going to work out with him."

"He kept you out for two days and now you're breaking up with him?" Mum's unimpressed face waited for my reply.

"Yes," I said.

Mum let out a long sigh and I cleared the dirty dishes away and excused myself upstairs.

Before making my way to the shower I took my phone out of my back pocket where it had miraculously stayed through the whole ordeal and found the hundreds of calls and texts that awaited me.

After Jayne got a call from my mum, she had obviously spread the word to the whole group as I had many messages from each of them checking if I was okay and trying to figure out where I was. There was also a message from Liam, but I was too nervous to look at that.

I sent each of my friends a quick message saying "sorry my mum scared you all, it was just a misunderstanding. I'm fine." Then I put my phone down and made my way into the bathroom.

Anxiety gripped my insides and pulled them into a tight knot. Would anything happen if I didn't go back to the park? Or if he could somehow leave and he came for me? If he could conjure a cage out of thin air to put me in, who knew what else he could do? No, I assured myself. He'd told me he couldn't leave.

A decision formed in my mind as the glorious heat from the water hit my skin. I couldn't see Jeremy again.

Wrapped in a soft towel, I retreated from the bathroom and lay on top of my bed. My sleep-deprived mind told me everything would be better if I took a nap and slept away the bad feelings, but my anxiety-riddled body told me to stay awake. Just in case.

Peeking at my phone I found several messages from my friends asking me where I had been and what had happened. I knew I shouldn't keep ignoring them but I couldn't tell them the truth. If I did, I took the risk that they would ask me to prove it, and when they couldn't enter Jeremy's Amusement Park I would look like a mad woman, or worse he could capture all of us. No, I had to keep this information to myself. We were all safer that way.

Laying in the comfort of my bed I finally looked at Liam's message. He wanted to meet that evening at a local bar.

Part of me knew it was a bad idea, he reminded me too much of Jeremy, and I needed to completely get rid of Jeremy from my life. But Liam was different to Jeremy, and I'd enjoyed talking to him.

I agreed to meet with him before I could convince myself that I shouldn't.

I thought about my summer so far. I had always pictured my last summer before university being a romantic, fun, adventure filled few weeks. Of course, breaking up with George had already ruined the first part of my imagined holiday but the rest had still been possible.

Now, I was caught up in some sort of twisted tale with a dead person and a magical amusement park. It was so ridiculous I still wasn't truly convinced of its existence myself. I couldn't seem to rid myself of the horrid feeling that none of it was real, and I had somehow dreamt it all up or was hallucinating as I wandered through the forest in the middle of the night by myself.

The worst part was that I still couldn't decide what I wanted to do about university. It was getting closer and I just wasn't sure if it was what I wanted. Jeremy hadn't helped at all, although the idea of getting as far away from him as I could was very appealing at the moment.

I knew that I couldn't see Jeremy again. I needed to stop myself from thinking about him, and forget I'd ever met him in the first place.

Forcing myself out of bed again, I found some clothes and pulled them onto my now dry body as I tried to muster up enough enthusiasm to put on some makeup and brush my hair. Pulling my curtains open I allowed golden rays to once again fill my room and delicious fresh air to waft through the open window.

"Mae," my mum's soft voice called through my door. "I'm just going to work now."

"Okay," I called back.

"Are you going to be here when I get home tonight?"

I took a deep breath in and let out an amused sigh. "Yes, Mum."

# Chapter 22

I wandered round the house lost for what to do with myself while I waited for the day to pass by and for the night to follow until I could finally talk to Liam. I wished I could force myself into the daylight but some part of me felt safer inside, like no one could see me.

I made myself a snack of fried egg on toast and another deliciously welcoming coffee and sat on the sofa finally looking through the messages from my friends and deleting the hundreds of missed calls from my parents the night before.

I scoffed at the completely unfeeling message from George. It was almost as if we had never dated in the first place.

I was sure he had seemed a lot more caring and intelligent two years ago when we had first gotten together. We had already known each other a little from school before George had ever asked me out, however, it was the summer before sixth form that we had started to spend quality time together and I really got to know him better. At least at the time I felt as though I had gotten to know him well.

Perhaps during the year and a half we had dated he had changed a lot more than I had realised, and perhaps I had changed as well. Although, I liked to think I had matured a bit better than George.

A fast, hard knocking came from the front door and I quickly got up to investigate who could be so desperate to be let in. A frustrated looking Jayne shook her head at me as I held the door open for her. Her hair was curly even while it was still damp and her face was fresh with no makeup covering her skin.

She stomped into the living room before turning around with her hands on her hips, imitating my mum's disapproval.

"What do you have to say for yourself then?" Her left eyebrow lifted high on her forehead and she pursed her lips expectantly.

"What do you mean?" I asked with a smirk as I took a seat as if readying myself for her lecture.

"I had your mother calling me up in a panic at midnight because you hadn't been home in two nights and you're going to tell me you don't know what I'm talking about?" She positioned herself on the arm of the sofa in an authoritative stance. "Where were you, Mae? And why haven't you been talking to me recently? Is it because you've been with that Jeremy guy you told me about?"

A sadness drew her eyebrows together and her lips dropped into a pout. Seeing a wet glisten take over her eyes I realised just how much I had been neglecting our friendship, and how much Jayne must really care.

I said the only thing I could think of that would explain my absence from her life. "We actually ended things. Me and Jeremy that is."

Jayne's eyebrows were hiding nothing of her true opinions on that day and they shot back up quickly and then together in an angry realisation.

"Are you serious? You've been bailing on me and putting us all through the loop for a guy you're not even with anymore?"

Although we hadn't been friends our whole lives, she was always so supportive and excited to hear my every update. Jayne had such a big overpowering personality that it was easy to let her life takeover everything else, but if ever I really needed to talk to her or take over the conversation for my own thing, she would take the time to listen.

"I'm sorry, I just got caught up in the moment. After everything with George, I was just happy to have someone else show an interest in me," I told her, embarrassed by my terrible excuse.

Jayne let her drying hair fall in front of her face while she thought about what I had said. The longer she remained silent the worse I felt, as if she deserved a much better friend than me. I started to wonder why she chose me in the first place, or why she'd stuck with me once she had gotten to know me.

"Well," Jayne finally said. "Do you want to tell me why you broke up? Are you okay?" She slipped down and sat properly on the seat next to me, lifting her leg onto the sofa so she could face me fully.

I searched my mind for something I could tell her. "He turned out to be a bit of a creep, honestly."

"Damn men."

Jayne stayed for a while longer and soon suggested we move into the back garden to enjoy the sun shine while she updated me on her week. I took a deep breath and checked over the garden for any spots someone could be hiding in and tried to slow my heartbeat before joining her.

I tried my best to listen to her talk about Tommy and how they had squabbled again about university and how they were going to make their relationship work so far apart but something kept dragging my attention away. First it was a shadow that looked like a man but turned out to be a bird on one of the low hanging branches of our rose bush, then it was a voice by my ear, but when I whipped around to catch the culprit I found only the whisper of the wind.

I tried to nod along as Jayne told me about the disappointing games night they had tried to have, the guys all started playing computer games instead of cards and Jayne didn't have the mental capacity to deal with zombies and shooting.

Even with all my efforts to stay focused on what my best friend had to tell me about her life I couldn't stop my mind from wandering into a terrible daydream, picturing the dark cage far away from any life, too far for anyone to hear me screaming. I could still hear Jeremy's footsteps as he raced to catch up with me when I escaped. What would he have done if he had caught me?

The memory of the cold hard ground against my shaking body flashed over my skin as I sat on the patio outside, and I jumped up so quickly Jayne asked me what was wrong. I told her it was cold and I wanted a cushion to sit on. Jayne of course knew I was lying; she was sitting on the same stone patio as me and she could feel where the sun had warmed it up herself. But she didn't call me out on the lie, just looked at me with a funny expression.

Jayne left when she noticed I was barely able to keep my eyes open, with the tiredness of the two sleepless nights finally getting to me. The warmth of the sun made me think of my lovely warm, cosy bed and I longed for my duvet around me.

My legs just about managed to make it to my bed before I allowed the tiredness to take over my body and my mind to become one with the world of sleep.

My mind remained dark as I slept that day. The cold metal bars of Jeremy's cage surrounded me once again, and I helplessly screamed for help, but no noise left my throat. I was surrounded by pitch black, the lights from the park were nowhere to be seen and silence pressed onto my head.

"Mae." I jumped at the sound of Jeremy's voice behind me. I spun round only to see more of nothing. My heart beat so loudly in my ears, I wondered if I would even hear him if he spoke again.

"Come back, Mae. I won't be angry."

"Where are you?" I tried to say.

"I am with you. You can be with me if you come back to the park. I will look after you," the voice said calmly. It sounded as though it was coming from everywhere, but I couldn't see him anywhere.

"No!" I shouted, holding my hands over my ears.

"You won't have to stay in a cage if you promise to stay."

"Go away!" Suddenly my waking mind mixed with my dreaming mind. It didn't feel like a dream, it felt as real as it had visiting the park. But if it was a dream, I could leave, I thought to myself. He couldn't get to me if I was awake. Wake up! I begged myself. Wake up! Wake up! Wake up!

I woke up feeling as if I hadn't really slept at all, I felt as though I had been in some kind of limbo.

My head lifted quickly off the pillow as I realised it was the front door opening and closing that had woken me. Determined not to let my mum know I had slept for most of the day while she had been at work, I jumped up and ran to the bathroom to splash some cold, refreshing water over my face.

"Mae," my mum called up the stairs. "Mae."

"Hi, Mum," I said casually, as I wandered down the stairs towards her waiting figure, as if I hadn't been unconscious only one minute before. "How was work?"

"Fine, thank you," she said. Was that relief I noticed when she saw me. "Have you eaten yet?"

I glanced over my mum's shoulder at the clock in the living room to discover it was five already. "Not yet," I said.

"Dad's working late tonight so would you like to have something together? I picked up a shepherd's pie from the shop, we could share it if you like." Mum put her leather handbag down on the side table by the door and made her way to the kitchen with her carrier bag.

"Let me make it, Mum," I said, trying to get back into her good books. She handed me the bag and I took out the shepherd's pie and pierced the film lid before placing it in the oven.

"It won't be as good as a homemade pie, but I felt like something easy tonight," my mum confessed as she made us both a glass of orange squash.

"Stressful day at work?" I asked, concerned at her lack of energy. My mum very rarely allowed herself an "easy" dinner, and didn't like to show when she was feeling rundown or under the weather.

"Not really, it was just busy today, and I didn't sleep much the last couple of nights."

"I'm so sorry about that, mum," I told her, knowing that it was my fault she hadn't slept.

"Never mind that now," mum said, waving her hand over the matter. "Let's just have a nice rest of the summer, shall we?"

"Deal," I said. I removed the rest of the shopping out of her carrier bag and put each of the items away, instant coffee, hand soap, and a bag of carrots. It was a strange mix, but seemed to be all things mum had decided she couldn't live without until the next weekly shop.

That evening mum put on some gentle music and sat on the left-hand side of the sofa while I sat on the right-hand side while I waited for it to be time to meet with Liam. When she opened her book, which she kept at easy reach on the coffee table, I decided to stay in her company. Mum was more of a reader than dad and often took the time to have some peace and quiet and to immerse herself in whatever book she had on the go at the time. As much as I had tried, I had never been able to quite pick up the same enthusiasm for reading as she had, and I would often excuse myself and do my own thing as to not disturb her silence. This time, I took out my phone and began to scroll through social media.

Over the last week or so it felt as if I had barely looked at my phone at all, which was probably a good thing, I realised as I looked through post after post from people I was barely even friends with and rarely spoke to.

I soon decided to give up on looking at the endless supply of selfies and people bragging about how well their summer was going and instead decided to look up more information about Jeremy's situation.

"Can spirits move on if they don't want to?" I Googled. What came up in answer to my question was an article about evil spirits and how to exorcise them from your house, and I wondered suddenly if Jeremy was evil.

The whole time I had spent with Jeremy, getting to know him and getting to know his amusement park, I had not once thought of him as evil. Even when he had trapped me in a cage, I had not considered that there could have been any truly malicious intent on his part.

I tried to remember anything Jeremy had said since I had first met him that I may have misinterpreted in my naive belief that he just needed helping. But nothing came to mind.

The more I thought of every interaction I'd had with Jeremy the more my heart began to speed up. It had all seemed so normal at the time. But it hadn't been, of course. What kind of spell had I been under to accept everything at face value like that?

Allowing a deep breath to fill my lungs, I let it out slowly as I tried to squash my concerns. My mum looked up briefly from her book but obviously decided I didn't look in any real distress because she soon looked back down at the page in her hand.

"Fancy a cup of tea?" I asked her, looking for something else to occupy my mind.

"That would be lovely, thank you," she said, without looking up from her novel.

My head spun as I watched the water bubble in the clear side panel of the kettle. Nerves were beginning to burn my stomach again as I thought of going out that evening. At least I would be with other people.

I tried to keep a positive mindset, telling myself that Jeremy couldn't leave the park, but that still didn't calm me.

As I poured boiling water into two matching mugs containing Camomile tea bags, I hoped that the delicious calming nature of the herbal tea would settle my shaking hands enough to allow me to seem normal when I met with Liam.

I took mum her tea and then brought mine to my bedroom where I made myself comfortable on top of my duvet and in front of the first cheesy romance I found. My head was in no place to be fully concentrating on a film that required proper attention and I didn't have long until I would be leaving.

I tried to dispel any images of Jeremy from my mind, although I couldn't stop seeing his eyes through the curtain I had drawn across the events of the last two days. Even as I drank my herbal tea, I couldn't stop my left foot from jiggling up and down where I had crossed it over my right. My hands shook only a little as I lifted the hot mug up to my face and then back down again between each sip.

By the time I had calmed my nerves it was time to get ready.

I pulled a thin grey jacket over my loose floral cami top and straightened my simple silver necklace. I completed my outfit with a pair of black boots with chunky heels.

I told my mum I would be back by ten and then left the house before I could change my mind.

A different set of nerves began to swarm through my bones as the reality of meeting with Jeremy's brother once again set in. The positivity Liam talked about finding after hitting a low when the accident had happened was lovely to hear about. That was the kind of thinking I needed more of now to stop myself from going back to Jeremy.

A golden sky sat low over my head and the evening warmth gusted through my hair. Walking through town I squashed my nerves lower down into my stomach and headed straight for the bar. This was the kind of normality I needed after my summer had started so strangely. Plenty of people were already filing through the door when I arrived, not anywhere near the amount I knew would arrive later in the evening. I hoped there would be a space available, I had arrived a little early and planned to find somewhere quiet to wait for Liam.

"Mae," Liam's voice called to me from a table on the far side. "You're early."

"So are you," I said. I took my bag off my shoulder and placed it on the chair next to mine as I sat opposite Liam.

The bar was the nicest one our town had to offer, but with it being a small town there weren't a lot of choices in the first place. It had an industrial feel to it, with fairy lights and fake plants dotted artfully around the room.

"How are you?" Liam asked me as he looked right into my dark eyes with his own emerald ones, which seemed to glow brightly even in the low lighting of the bar.

We exchanged niceties and then Liam offered to get us some drinks, hurrying away to the bar before he would let me pay for my own. After spending a few nights with Jeremy, I was somehow surprised to see that Liam had changed his clothes. He wore a nice neat shirt with plain black jeans.

Liam returned, placing my beer in front of me and took his seat opposite. I thanked him and insisted I would buy the next round. We both took a few sips of our drinks before either of us said anything. Now I was there I was finding it hard to think of what to say to him, I couldn't stop seeing Jeremy is Liam's features.

"I forgot to ask the other day, where are you going to university?" Liam asked before I had a chance to think of anything.

Thankful for having something to talk about I told him I would be going to Lincoln.

"I go to Nottingham, it's not far from Lincoln," he said.

"Maybe we'll bump into each other then," I laughed.

After I explained that I hadn't spent much time in the area and had only really been there for my interview and university tour, Liam told me about his favourite places. Apparently, he had explored the area quite thoroughly during his first year at university, especially during the times he was avoiding socialising.

"I'd love to give you the tour some time," Liam said shyly.

"That would be nice," I said, trying not to over-analyse the fact he was making plans for months in the future. He was assuming that he would still want to see me by then. What did he think this meeting was?

"How have you been enjoying your summer so far? Are you glad to be home?" I asked.

Liam's grin was a little more one sided than Jeremy's, but it was just as charming.

"It started off a little dull to be honest," he admitted. "Meeting you for coffee was a much needed high."

"It was?" I asked, disbelievingly.

"Of course. I really enjoyed talking to you."

I thought back to the conversations we'd had over coffee and remembered that it hadn't all been about Jeremy, we had talked about more than just that, he had asked a lot about me and we had gotten to know each other a small amount. Warmth spread across my cheeks and I tried to hide it by looking at my drink.

"I had a good time too," I admitted.

We had another few drinks while we talked more about ourselves, mostly I asked Liam about himself.

While Liam talked I noticed things about him, differences between him and Jeremy. Liam held himself more confidently, with a straighter spine and a higher neck. His eyes, although as beautiful and bright, weren't as wide as Jeremy's. He seemed to have a much more mature and educated view on life. It was refreshing to talk to someone with real world experiences, someone who had seen something and somewhere other than the little town I had grown up in.

Liam made me feel excited to leave and start on the next stage of my life, somewhere new. He encouraged me to talk about what life could be like, going from his own great experiences.

"Do your parents visit you much?" I asked.

"A little," Liam said. "It can be a little difficult fitting them both in because they have to visit separately. But it is nice to share it with them."

"It must be difficult for you with your parents separated."

"It's easier than when they were together," Liam admitted. "At least now I'm not listening to them snap at each other and bicker constantly. They both seem happier apart."

I thought about my own parents, wondering if they would ever separate, and how that might make me feel. I couldn't imagine my happy, cuddly parents ever splitting up, they showed more affection for each other than any other parents I knew.

"Were they always unhappy?" I asked.

"I don't think so," Liam said shyly. He didn't appear to mind the topic. "When I was a kid, we were always going out at the weekends on family adventures. But I guess they just grew apart." He took a deep breath. "Anyway, let's talk about something a little more interesting. Tell me more about yourself."

"There's not much to tell."

"I don't believe that."

"Pretty normal family, I'm an only child, my parents are still together, and there's not much other than that."

Liam smirked as he finished off his drink. "How about, I'll go and get us another round, and while I'm gone you think of something a little more interesting to tell me about yourself. I can tell there's more to you than you're letting on."

Panic suddenly set in as I watched Liam chatting casually to the barman, what could I tell him? He wasn't really putting me on the spot but I did have a deadline for this question, and that's what had made my mind suddenly go blank, forgetting every interesting fact about myself.

I couldn't stop my wandering mind from trying to picture what Liam might have been like before the accident. He was twelve for starters, so he probably wouldn't have been hanging out at a bar and laughing with the friendly barman. Had he always been so kind natured or had that come from the reality of losing his brother?

By the time Liam sat opposite me again I realized I had spent the whole time thinking about him and forgetting to think about myself.

"Okay, how about you tell me why you cut your hair short?" Liam said casually.

"How do you know I haven't always had it short?" I asked, attempting a mysterious drawl to my voice.

"I may have looked you up, and I noticed that the short hair is relatively new."

Liam had looked me up. What did that mean? Well, I had looked him up too so I couldn't say much to that.

I took a deep breath, preparing myself to let him into the embarrassing reason behind my hair cut. "I was going through a breakup." I put my head in my hands. "I know, I know, I'm a cliche!"

Liam's ivy eyes swept over my hair slowly, finally landing back on my eyes. "I like it better this way, going from the photos that is."

I couldn't help but allow a smile to spread over my warming cheeks. "Good, because I was thinking of keeping it this way."

When Liam placed his hand around his pint glass, I suddenly wondered what it would feel like for him to run his fingers through my hair. Quickly I looked away from his hand and squashed the thought out of my mind, telling myself I was only thinking it because I was feeling lonely after finding out how wrong my feelings for Jeremy were.

As the night went on, I stopped noticing Jeremy in Liam, and started seeing him as a completely different, and exciting person. He laughed a lot, and he was flirtatious in a way that I couldn't remember Jeremy ever being. Liam had a lot to say when you got him talking, he asked about me an equal amount, eagerly listening to everything I said. The way he paid attention to me talking made me feel important and shy at the same time.

I couldn't remember how much we drank, the drinks seemed to just appear in front of me one by one, by the time I'd finished one drink another one was in my hand, and I was lifting it to my mouth.

Before I knew it, the sun was high in the sky and I was waking up in my bed.

# Chapter 23

The sun glared viciously through my bedroom window when I finally opened my eyes the next morning. Groaning, I pulled the duvet high above my head and curled into a tight ball, the pulsing in my head telling me not to get up yet. I didn't fight it, I just followed its instructions and allowed myself to fall back to sleep.

A couple of hours later I slowly squinted my eyes open to see that the sun was still up and pouring through my thin curtains. Silence filled the house and I was sure my parents had to be at work already.

Memories of the night before came rolling into my mind and a dark feeling crept under my duvet and over my skin.

After demanding Liam walk me home at nine-forty-five, I had miraculously arrived home within my mum's curfew. I'd gone straight to bed, hoping for a good night's sleep, but had found myself back in Jeremy's Amusement Park.

The disorientating lights had spun around and around until I found Jeremy and was able to focus my eyes on his face.

"Are you alright," Jeremy had asked me with concern as I stumbled over to him.

"I saw Liam tonight," I slurred, as he held me steady with one hand on each of my arms. I had been so numb I had barely felt his touch at all, but I had still flinched at his hold on me.

"Is he here?" Jeremy had asked. Only now in the light of day did I realise his expression had been anticipation.

"No." I didn't know why I was talking to him at all. Even in the dream my intoxicated mind knew it was wrong. Why was I even there?

"You should go, Mae," Jeremy said sternly. "Sleep off whatever came over you and then join me here. Tomorrow."

Regret fought with the disappointment. Knowing I should never have come in the first place I ran from Jeremy without another word. I'd hoped he would be happy to see me, I'd hoped that even in my drunken state he would have smiled at me in the cheeky toothy way he often had.

But he hadn't. Jeremy had taken one look at the state of me and sent me away from his perfect playful amusement park, and home to wallow in my own stupidity.

I'd woken up with a jolt as my dream self ran into the forest.

My phone vibrated sharply on the table next to my bed, distracting me from the humiliating memory and I reached over to pick it up. I had to hold the phone close to my face to read the message from Liam.

"I haven't had that much fun or drunk that much in ages. How are you feeling this morning?"

I smiled at the message not yet sure I could form a proper response. My mouth felt as though it had been glued shut, and my head pounded. I put the phone down and took a long drink from the glass of water I found next to my bed where I must have put it the night before.

It felt like an hour had passed before I picked up my phone again to reply to Liam's message.

"Thanks for the good night, but you'll pay for this hangover I've got."

"How about I take you out for brunch to make up for it?"

Unexpected excitement filled my chest as I thought about seeing him again. I checked the time, it was already eleven. It would be closer to lunch time by the time I was able to roll out of bed and force myself into a hot shower.

"I can meet you at 12.30?"

I put my phone down after Liam chose a cafe in town and rolled onto my side, hugging the duvet closer to my aching body, telling myself I should get up over and over again until I finally did.

Slowly, I hung my bare legs off the side of my mattress and held my head in my hands, willing the spinning room to slow down enough for me to stand. Eventually I heaved myself onto my feet and made my way to the bathroom.

Allowing the water to heat up significantly before stepping under it, I washed as much of the hangover off my skin as I could. I wondered if it was really a hangover affecting me or was it the lack of sleep?

While letting the heavenly water run through my hair and down my back I stared at the shower wall in front of me. Even though I was physically staying away from the park it was still in my dreams, preventing me from getting any real rest. That was a disturbing development.

It had only been a day since I had seen Jeremy but the guilt was beginning to burn my stomach. I couldn't help but think how lonely he must be, by himself again.

I shook my head, and with it shook out the feelings of guilt. Jeremy had brought this upon himself by putting me in a cage and leaving me there for two nights.

I wrapped a towel tight around my body and searched my wardrobe for an appropriate outfit, trying hard to not look as bad as I felt. It looked like it was going to be another hot day, although the humidity again gave the daunting impression of a storm heading our way.

Choosing a pair of light denim shorts and another loose strappy top, I dressed quickly, leaving myself with only a little time left to apply some simple makeup.

My head felt heavy and acid burned my empty stomach but I persevered and forced myself to leave the house and enter the force field of heat outside.

The rest of the town seemed to have been up for much longer than I had, with cheery people swarming the streets and soaking in the rays of sunshine. A smiling family passed me on the street with a young girl chatting away happily to a gurgling baby in his pram while their parents discussed where to get lunch.

Hearing the mention of lunch, I checked the time worrying I was late meeting Liam for our brunch, and hurried my feet to get to the cafe before Liam became tired of waiting for me.

The sweet relief of the cafe's aircon hit my clammy skin as I entered, and I felt myself wishing I would never have to leave again. Spotting Liam only just taking a seat at a small table on the opposite side of the cafe to the door, I made my way to him.

"Hi, I ordered you a coffee. I didn't know what you liked so I got you a black coffee with milk on the side just in case," Liam said when I reached the table.

"Perfect," I sighed with relief.

"How are you feeling?" he asked, his beautiful eyes searching my exhausted face.

"Like I really needed this coffee," I laughed. "You?"

"Me too. I haven't drunk that much since I've been back from uni."

I groaned with pleasure as I felt the delicious hot coffee touch my tongue and slide into my stomach.

"Death is a good way of describing how I feel," I joked. Liam laughed, but it was different to his usual fun-loving laugh, this one was more of polite uncomfortable laugh. I realised my insensitive mistake sucking at the air between us. "I'm so sorry," I said with utter embarrassment.

"That's okay," Liam said looking down at his drink. The noise from the tables surrounding ours almost hid the awkward silence between us. I decided with the subject already hanging uncomfortably in the air I might as well just continue the awkward conversation and see what Liam really thought. "Do you believe in life after death?"

I could barely lift my eyes from my coffee, unwilling to see Liam's disapproving expression. But it seemed as though I hadn't offended him too much as he replied with a light voice. "I like to think that Jeremy is in heaven, if such a place exists."

"What if he wasn't?" I asked, glancing up quickly to see his quizzical expression and then quickly let my eyes fall back down. When he didn't reply I continued. "What if his spirit was stuck or-."

"Let's not talk about this," Liam said sadly.

"I just-."

"Mae, please," Liam begged; his voice was so heartbreaking that I couldn't bring myself to continue.

Neither of us spoke, the seriousness of the situation setting in. I shouldn't have said anything. Even if Liam could see and talk to Jeremy, would he really be able to go through the loss of his brother a second time?

"Let's get something to eat," Liam said letting out a long breath and forcing a smile to spread back over his lips.

I agreed, almost too embarrassed to speak again.

We ordered and then Liam began a new conversation, casual and light hearted, and soon the mention of the afterlife and of Jeremy was forgotten. My mistake appeared to have been forgiven and we even began to laugh again. I seemed to find myself laughing often with Liam.

"Where are you staying while you're back?" I asked.

"I'm staying with my mum," Liam said as he took a bite from his bacon bap.

"Is it nice spending some more time with her while you're here?"

"It is nice when I actually see her. But she works a lot and when she's not working, she spends a lot of time with this new man she's seeing." Liam said it so matter-of-factly like he didn't care much.

"Don't you mind?" I asked curiously.

"Not really, it's been a while since our family has bothered with quality time together. It's more like short and sweet visits."

"Have you met the man she's seeing?"

"I have. He's nice enough, seems to genuinely be interested in my mum which is more than I can say for some of the other men she's dated." The way Liam talked it was as though he had gotten so used to not seeing his mum and her dating that it didn't faze him at all.

"Well as long as you don't really dislike him."

"Not at all, I just haven't had enough time to really get to know him yet." A cheeky grin spread over his face. "Does mean I have the house to myself most of the time."

I laughed. "Throwing a lot of mad parties, are you?"

"Oh yes, many parties," Liam joked. "Honestly, it's just nice having the quiet and not having to worry about making conversation first thing in the morning or if I come home after having a few too many drinks."

"I get that," I grinned. "My parents always want to have serious conversations before I've even had a coffee."

We finished our brunch, my hangover significantly satisfied, and then ordered another coffee each. Around us the hungry customers at each of the tables kept changing but we remained comfortably seated at our little table for two. Time moved too quickly with Liam and I found myself wishing it would slow down so we would have more of it together. Once I had stopped thinking about Jeremy, Liam was very easy to talk to and he was interesting. I found myself wondering if he thought the same about me or if one night of drinking and a brunch might be as much as he could take of me.

I watched the way Liam's smile seemed to pick up more on the left and noticed the cute dimple it created. When his eyes lifted from his coffee and found mine firmly searching his face, he kept contact with me for several seconds and I noticed odd auburn flecks mixed into the beautiful green.

I felt his gaze remain on me even when I lowered my eyes and pretended the hot blush on my cheeks wasn't as noticeable as it felt.

The large brass clock hanging over the counter told me it was nearly 5pm, and the coffee shop would be closing soon. A tightness pulled at my chest and I willed the clock to stop moving so we would have more time.

My eyes wandered down from the clock to where the young woman behind the counter was passing over a takeaway coffee cup. The man thanked her and turned around; his eyes locked on mine immediately. Neither of us moved for a second, then George's gaze slipped from mine quickly onto Liam and then back again. I smiled politely hoping he would take the hint and leave.

"Hi, Mae." The smile did not quite reach George's lips as he stood by our table.

"Hi," I said, glancing only slightly to where I knew Liam was innocently watching our awkward exchange. "How are you?"

"Fine, thanks, haven't seen you much recently," George said, deliberately ignoring Liam.

"Sorry, I've been... Um... Busy." What could I say? I had been busy, busy visiting a dead guy in the middle of the night, busy getting to know his living brother during the day, but also, I was avoiding them, avoiding my friends. Jayne had texted me a few times since we'd last hung out and I had replied with non-specific answers.

George's eyes finally met with Liam's and he introduced himself. Liam replied by standing and shaking his hand, kindly suggesting George join us.

"They're about to close anyway," George said as he declined the offer. I silently thanked the brass clock for ignoring my last prayer and continuing to move.

"We should probably get going then so they can clear our table," Liam chuckled. I rose out of my chair without a word. I shouldn't have felt guilty that my ex-boyfriend had spotted me out with another man, because we weren't really out, it wasn't a date. Was it?

I left the two guys standing together awkwardly while I made my way to the counter to pay for our meals and coffee. Only one other table was still hanging around now, they were lucky to be sitting away from us so they didn't have to witness our struggling conversation with George. Even from where I stood at the counter, I could hear Liam trying to make polite conversation with

George while he refused to say more than one-word answers.

"Shall we go?" I said not really to either of them but also to both of them.

Outside the cafe George lingered around us as we said goodbye.

"I'll walk you home if you like," Liam suggested eagerly.

"I'm going that way anyway, I can walk her," George said. I desperately tried to apologize to Liam with my eyes.

"Well, I'll see you again soon then," Liam said looking directly at me, his eyes lingering long enough to suggest something.

"See you soon," I said with a smile.

Turning away from Liam I allowed a few seconds for him to get a safe distance away before speaking to George. "You know I can walk myself home, right?"

We walked a few steps without a word and I continued wondering why he was still walking with me in the opposite direction to his own house.

"We've all been worried about you, Mae. I just wanted to make sure you're alright. That's all," George said, lowering his voice, the harsh tone falling away.

"I'm fine. Really." I wondered if my disappearance had caused more concern than I had expected.

"Look, I'm sorry it's been awkward between us recently. If you want to hang out with everyone without me, I can stay home a bit, give you some time with them."

Surprised by what George said, it took me a few seconds to think of a reply. "It's really fine." I said.

"Okay." George turned the opposite way to walk home without another word. We had barely had a full conversation since we'd broken up, but in this quick exchange I could tell that at one point he had really cared about me.

# Chapter 24

Dark menacing clouds were forming over my head by the time I made it home, appearing quickly as if in a rush. The humidity stuck sharply in the air and a layer of sweat coated my skin.

Closing the door slowly behind myself as I entered the house I felt as though my mood had turned with the weather. Storms were beautiful in theory but for me they always came with a slither of worry that sat in my chest like a stubborn rock. And this time, that rock looked remarkably like Jeremy.

I imagined Jeremy in his amusement park while the rain beat down on all the games and rides. I wondered if the rain would reach Jeremy, or if it would forever be dry just as it was forever nighttime.

Only my dad was home that evening, my mum working the evening shift at work. "I thought we would have pizza if that's okay with you?" he said.

"Sure," I replied, glad for the comfort food and company.

Dad put the pizza in the oven and then sat next to me on our comfy sofa and began looking for something to watch on the television. It wasn't often that I spent the evening with my parents but I felt like having the company that night.

My phone vibrated in my pocket and a strange excitement filtered through me when I saw Liam's name.

"I'm guessing that was your ex then?"

"Yeah, sorry about that."

"No worries. I had a nice day with you."

"Me too. Think we left at just the right time, looks like a storm is coming in."

"True. Although I don't think I'd mind being stuck in a storm with you."

A smile pulled at the corners of my lips and I thought hard about how to reply to Liam's flirtatious text. A small part of me couldn't remove the image of Jeremy from my mind, even after everything he had done, I still felt a stab of guilt in my stomach. I knew there was nothing wrong with me talking to Liam, or even if I were to return his flirtatious comments. I didn't owe Jeremy anything.

He wasn't really alive, he wasn't really available for dating, and the more I thought about it the more I wondered if that had even been on Jeremy's mind at all. He hadn't tried to flirt with me the way Liam had. Occasionally he gave me compliments but mostly we just played games. I wondered if that was because he knew nothing could ever come from our having a relationship. But if that were the truth why did he keep asking me to stay? Why had he been so upset when I left every night?

It occurred to me that Jeremy's attention to me had come just at the time I needed someone to distract me from my lingering feelings for my ex-boyfriend. Perhaps I had misjudged the interest he'd shown me.

After a long thought about how best to reply I finally decided to follow Liam's lead.

"I think I might quite like that too."

Until the pizza was out of the oven I continued to text with Liam. His mum was out with her boyfriend that evening and he was having cheese on toast for dinner by himself. I wished I could be spontaneous and invite myself to his house to hide from the storm together, but an unwelcome voice in my head was telling me I was spending too much time with him. Liam didn't invite me round either.

I told him how I was sharing a large spicy chicken pizza with my dad while we watched Indiana Jones, which was one of my dad's favourites. "It's a classic," he told me every few months when he put it on again.

Rain hammered down heavily all evening and right into the night. I didn't feel like being by myself but when my mum arrived home and curled up next to my dad, I excused myself to my room, away from their cutesy kisses. Leaving my window open a crack to let the fresh damp air into my room I sat down on top of my duvet and put on another film.

"What are you watching?" Liam asked, I told him I was watching To All The Boys I've Loved Before ignoring the embarrassment of the fact it was a girly romance. "Found it, I'll watch it with you," he texted a minute later.

As the film went on, we discussed the cheesy plot line and even cheesier acting. I could tell it wasn't the kind of film that Liam would normally choose for himself but his commentary of the flawed story and doomed relationship made me see the film through a new set of eyes, and laugh at things I wouldn't normally see as humorous.

When the film finished, I said a reluctant goodnight to Liam and lay only half way under my duvet as I felt the cool outside air on my bare skin. I listened as the rain continued to fall heavily around my window. Knowing that Liam was only on the other end of the phone, watching the same film as me, made me feel less lonely and exposed.

Tiredness took hold of my limbs but my loud thoughts kept my mind from drifting off to sleep. Liam's cheerful smile shot in front of my eyes and his flirtatious comments swam into my ears. I tried desperately to fight the feelings taking over my chest. I had been down this road before with a Brown brother and I didn't know if it was a good idea.

Even with that in mind I couldn't stop the smile on my face from growing when I thought about how he had said good night to me that evening. "Goodnight beautiful," he had said. I hadn't replied after that, letting his words soak slowly into me.

I wondered if Liam really felt the same way or if he was just flirting. Perhaps I was thinking too far into it and he was merely enjoying his summer home from university.

When the morning brightly rolled through my window, my eyes were already open, barely even noticing the lack of sleep I'd had that night.

With my eyes opened I saw Liam's happy, charming face, but when I closed them all I could see was Jeremy. His fierce eyes waiting for my return to the park, the cage next to him, ready to capture me again.

I picked up my phone and disappointment settled in as I saw I had no new messages. After receiving a goodnight message from Liam, I had hoped it would be followed by a good morning one.

I lay on my back for a few minutes wondering if Liam was even awake yet, and if he was, what he could be doing that prevented him from texting me? I imagine him sitting at the dinner table drinking coffee and eating toast. Would his mum be back already?

I picked up my phone and sent him a message before I could think twice. "Morning."

Rolling out of bed quickly before I could obsess too much over whether or not Liam might reply, I made my way over to the open window.

Outside the rain had stopped and the sky was beginning to clear letting the morning sun shine through. Fresh, clean air made its way into my system and I felt a calmness come over me. The stress and excitement that had been building in my chest washed away with a gust of delicious air.

"Morning," Liam replied after only a couple of minutes.

I sat on the edge of my bed desperately searching my mind for a reply. "Did you make it through the storm?"

"Just about, you?" Liam replied.

"Me too."

"Glad to hear it."

"What are you doing later?"

"Whatever you want me to be doing." I could hear Liam saying it even through the message.

"I'll let you know." I left my phone on the bed and made my way to the bathroom. It was my turn to decide what we were going to be doing and I thought of all the things we had to do in our little town.

I had to choose the appropriate outfit for plans I hadn't fully decided on yet and that was a difficult decision. I kept it simple with denim shorts and a little summery top, covered with a thin cardigan in case the storm had left a chill in the air.

As I poured a hot cup of coffee my mind raced with possibilities. I wondered whether or not my plans were going to be considered a date or just a friendly hangout, and then I wondered if my plans should reflect what I was hoping for. But what was I hoping for?

We had been for coffee twice and out for drinks once so something outside was probably a good choice this time, especially with the emerging sunshine.

I texted Liam and told him where to meet me after lunch, giving myself time to get some makeup on and have something to eat with my parents.

# Chapter 25

Quacking ducks dived at the seeds spraying from the small hands of a young girl at the side of the canal, surrounded by birds while her mum held tightly onto her hand.

More families dropped their offerings in various spaces beside the water, wide grins pasted across their faces. Laughter vibrated from the children.

Standing back on the wide path I let others pass while I waited to meet up with Liam, I had arrived early hoping to get my thoughts in order before he arrived. I still had not decided what exactly I was doing.

Liam seemed to have been flirting with me since the day we met, but I could hardly come out and ask what his intentions were, especially as he was blissfully unaware of the real reason I had gotten in touch with him in the first place.

A refreshing, light gust of air sailed through my hair and over my warm skin, the midday sun was gleaming furiously from the sky.

I was just wondering if my face had already turned too red from the heat or if it was just that cute pink colour over my cheeks and nose when I felt a soft touch on my arm. Turning I spotted Liam's charming grin.

"Hi," he said. I couldn't help but notice that his skin was the same shade of red I imagined mine was.

"Hi," I replied, trying not to relish the feeling of his fingers on my arm. Liam was also wearing a t-shirt and shorts, but his outfit showed off significantly less skin than mine.

We started walking up the canal, sliding smoothly out of the way of the feasting birds and cheerful children. Walking single file made it hard to make any conversation, but after a few minutes we were away from the car park and the majority of the birds leaving more space for us to stand next to each other.

"Beautiful day," Liam commented. His arm rubbed smoothly against mine as he walked closely beside me.

I agreed hoping desperately that he didn't notice the beads of sweat forming around my face. Glancing up to quickly see his face I saw that his cheeks had continued to redden as well.

"There's a bit up here which is more shaded from the sun," I promised, more so to myself than to Liam.

We soon came to a crossroads; the first option was to continue straight ahead on the flat concrete path and the second option was to climb over a slightly rotting gate onto a grassy path leading into low hanging trees.

Liam let me climb over the gate first, offering his hand to help me lift my leg over. Curious to feel his hand in mine I thanked him and accepted his help even though I knew it would make it harder to climb over than if I had just used both hands to hold onto the fence.

His hand was warm, just as I had expected, and big enough to swallow mine whole. His hold on me felt strong and stable while I used it to leverage myself over the gate.

I waited on the other side as Liam confidently followed me over the fence, trying not to make it obvious that I was watching him.

"Have you been this way before?" I asked him.

"I don't think so," he replied, returning to stand close to me. "I didn't used to go for a lot of walks when I was living here."

A glorious shade covered our bodies and we slowed down to savour the relief from the heat. I could see the uneven path ahead was mostly covered in the shade from the trees and I prayed it remained that way. I didn't normally mind that kind of heat, but when I might want to come off as somewhat attractive I didn't want to chance Liam seeing me too red and sweaty.

"What did you used to do with your friends?" I ask curiously.

"We mostly just hung out in town or played ball games," he admitted.

"Don't you play ball games anymore?"

"Not so much," Liam said. "It's more about pubs and lengthy assignments nowadays."

He didn't sound too unhappy about the change of his hobbies.

Liam appeared to be thinking about something for a while before he went on. "I'd always wanted to play basketball with Jeremy but he was usually pretty busy with his team. When I was old enough to play properly, he had already... you know... So, me and my mates just messed around with it to pass the time."

I nodded, not wanting to think about Jeremy too much.

A large muddy puddle awaited us ahead. This path was often too flooded to walk on in the winter, and it seemed the rain had been heavy enough the night before to have the same effect now in the summer.

Liam tactically stepped with one leg at the very edge of the puddle and then jumped the rest of the way. He turned back to me as if beckoning me to follow in his footsteps.

"I'm not sure I'm going to be able to make it across like you," I laughed nervously, taking as long a step as I could across the side of the puddle, not quite making it to the footprint Liam had left. Mud enclosed around my light plimsoll shoes. With only a thin tree branch in reaching distance I grabbed at it to stop myself from falling further into the mud while I pulled my foot free of the wet that was soaking through to my skin.

Taking another long step towards the side where Liam was waiting for me, arms outstretched ready to help me over the last step. Just as I reached for Liam's outstretched hand, I felt the mud beneath my feet slip and I missed Liam's hand altogether.

Before I knew it Liam had dived forward and had his arms around my waist pulling me back into a standing position and out of the mud before I could fall all the way down.

"I got you," he said, his arms remaining tightly around me, holding me steady.

"Thank you," I said shyly looking down at my now brown shoes. I glanced across at Liam's which after making it safely across the muddy puddle to begin with were now as brown as mine. "Sorry about your shoes," I said stepping away from his hold.

"That's alright, they weren't really clean to begin with," he laughed.

Dirty wet mud squelched between my toes and I willed myself not to ruin my time with Liam by letting on about my uncomfortable shoes.

The walk I had chosen was not a long one and would only take a couple of hours to finish the route completely. Midway round the walk was an old wooden bench hidden back slightly in between two thick trees. Liam led me off the path when he spotted it and took a seat on the warm wood.

Liam's whole body turned to face me as if preparing for me to tell him something incredible. His knee lifted slightly onto the seat and he rested his right arm over the back. I turned awkwardly to imitate his position.

"This is a nice walk," he said softly, his eyes reflected the bright glow from the sun as he looked down at me. The auburn flecks stood out in the bright daylight.

"It's nice on a day like this," I said, feeling as though he wasn't really listening.

Liam's warm hand tucked my short hair gently behind my ear, his fingers lingered on the side of my face for longer than I had expected and I felt my bottom lip anxiously slip between my teeth. Liam's hand slid smoothly from my ear to my jaw and under my chin, lifting my face to his.

His lips were warm and slow on my own surprised lips. At first, I didn't move, my back stiff with the shock of kissing someone new. When he didn't back away, I allowed myself to fall into the kiss, embracing the feeling of his affection.

I licked my lips as he moved away from me. "I've been wanted to do that since I noticed you in the café the morning we met."

"You have?" I said, unable to look away from his lips. With only one taste I wanted more.

"Of course," Liam said smoothly, moving his hand from my face and sliding it slowly down my arm. "Was it okay that I kissed you?"

"Yes," I said, without a doubt.

The tingling feeling of his lips on mine remained for the rest of the walk, persuading the wide grin on my face to go wasn't an easy task, and it appeared Liam was struggling with the same issue.

Liam's hand slipped smoothly around mine as we continued wandering under the shade of the leafy trees, and his fingered entwined with mine holding me firmly next to him.

We passed only one other group on our walk, a family with three children excitedly running rings around their parents. My hand remained comfortably in Liam's as we moved to walk single file so they could pass us easily and I wondered if to that family we looked like a couple on a romantic stroll together.

As we made our way closer towards the busy car park and large families throwing bird seeds and bread in the canal, I found myself wishing I had chosen a longer walk. Liam seemed to have slowed his pace considerably and I wondered if he too was hoping to spend more time with me. Options of how I could extend our time together swarmed my mind and I searched for a viable suggestion that would mean a quiet place Liam and I could be together without interruption.

"Do you fancy getting an ice cream?" Liam suggested casually.

"Sure," I agreed, eager to stop him from going home.

"Just one more thing before we go," Liam said, turning toward me once again and leaning quickly down to leave a delicious kiss on my lips. He smiled smugly and I wondered if I looked as spellbound as I felt.

He led me past the crowded families to a small ice cream van that was parked at the top of the car park, with several people already queuing in front of its serving window. I couldn't help but notice that Liam had begun to lean more on his right foot than his left as he walked slowly to the ice-cream van queue.

"What flavour do you want?" he asked, as we joined the line of people eagerly waiting for their sweet treat.

"Mint please," I said.

"Mint?" Liam questioned with a smirk.

"What's wrong with mint?"

"It's like eating iced toothpaste," Liam laughed with me.

"Well maybe I like the taste of toothpaste."

The queue moved forward and soon we were at the window ready to order. "Are you sure," Liam said sarcastically. He only removed his hand from mine long enough to pay for our ice cream and then promptly replaced his fingers between mine, steering me to a low wall guarding a flower patch where we sat close together to enjoy our refreshing ice cream.

"Are you okay?" I asked Liam, and pointed to his left leg.

"It's nothing," he assured me. "Since the accident, it's been a bit hard for me to walk too far."

"I'm so sorry!" I exclaimed, embarrassed by my thoughtlessness.

"No, it's really okay. I'm usually fine, it was just a longer walk than I had expected." It hit me again suddenly, how Liam was still living with the consequences from the accident, and would be for the rest of his life.

"How are you enjoying your frozen toothpaste?" Liam joked, after a long silence.

"Very much, thank you! So, what are your plans for the rest of the summer?"

I watched Liam's eyebrows furrow together slightly and his eyes wander into the distance as he thought about his answer. "I think that really depends on what your plans are?" He smiled flirtatiously. I grinned at him. I could almost forget everything else that was going on, I could forget Jeremy, I could forget my friends and I could forget my future just to feel the butterflies in my stomach that Liam caused.

I had forgotten how it felt to have a guy interested in me and for me to be interested back, to flirt and kiss and laugh together. George had been my first boyfriend and the only experience I had to compare to. And even though I'd thought I might never be happy again, after we broke up, I had to admit that this new relationship, if that's what it was, was even better.

# Chapter 26

I spent the next few days mostly with Liam and if I wasn't with him I was texting him. We watched movies together at his house, went for short walks, and one day we had a small picnic, consisting of prepackaged sandwiches from the supermarket and a bottle of orange juice each.

Although I'd been surprised by the kiss at first, since then I'd found myself longing for more. I realised that I enjoyed spending time with Liam, it didn't feel as childish as with Jeremy, it felt as if we were both adults in the real world with the daylight actually playing a part in our new relationship. Liam seemed interested in me all the time, and I thought of how Jeremy had only shown real interest between games or when I was asking him too many questions. Liam held a conversation for longer than Jeremy ever had, and I enjoyed speaking to him, and hearing what he had to say.

Liam had also made the choice to not work through the summer. He told me about his apprenticeship at a local veterinary practice in Nottingham where he worked two full days and one-half day during term time as well as attending lectures and completing assignments. Working there kept him busy and because of that he had decided not to work for the few weeks he would be home that summer.

At the back of my mind, I knew I should be worrying about Jeremy plaguing my dreams every night. I'd begun to avoid sleeping as much as I could, and I almost felt as though I were living in a haze of tiredness. Unable to function as smoothly as I normally would while my mind was being starved of much needed rest, I had become clumsy and often forgetful.

I couldn't ignore the difference between the relationship I'd thought I'd had with Jeremy and the one I had with Liam. Jeremy had never really been interested in me, and I always felt like I had to make up for something. With Liam, I could relax, he encouraged me move forward, and he never wanted anything from me.

Jayne asked me to join them a few times and each time I was already with Liam and told her I was busy. I noticed that invitations to hang out with my friends were becoming far less frequent and part of me felt disappointed, even though I knew it was all my fault.

"Is everything okay?" Liam asked when I kept checking my phone.

"It's just my friend, she wants me to go out with them." I rolled my eyes as I turned off my phone.

"We can go if you want," Liam said. "I'd like to meet your friends."

"Maybe next time," I said. "I'm enjoying just hanging out with you." I wanted nothing more than to show off Liam to Jayne and I wanted everyone to know I was happy. But a nagging voice at the back of my head told me not to introduce him to them until I knew for certain he wouldn't leave me.

I distracted Liam from his offer to meet my friends by showering him with playful kisses. He didn't seem to mind.

"Tell me about your parents," he said quietly, allowing his warm hand to glide softly over my exposed shoulder. Both our legs were crossed as we sat facing each other in the long grass of one of the overgrown farmer's fields. His hand slowly stroked down my arm until his fingers entwined with mine.

"There's not much more than what I've already told you," I said, barely able to think about anything other than his skin against mine.

"All you've said is that it's just the three of you. I know nothing else about them," Liam reasoned with me.

"Well, my mum is the manager of a café in town."

"That's great, which cafe?" Liam's casual, caring smile illuminated every other detail on his face.

"Mateo's Café."

Liam's glowing eyes widened a little as I saw him realise which cafe I was talking about. "I love that place. Isn't it a restaurant as well?"

I explained how it was converted into a restaurant in the evenings and how my mum often ended up working a double shift to help out.

"What about your dad?" Liam moved the conversation forward.

"He's an estate agent."

"Sounds like they both have pretty full-on jobs," Liam said. Understanding laced his voice, and I wondered if I also heard a little pity. He lifted my chin gently so my eyes were in line with his. "Does it bother you? That both your parents work so much."

I thought over his question and then let a smile grow shyly onto my lips. "Sometimes," I admitted. "But I admire how much they work, and I know they would do anything for me."

Liam's gaze wandered from mine and glanced at the tall grass around us, the colour of his eyes standing out beautifully from the dull, dehydrated greenery. "Must be nice to know how much your parents care about you."

"Are your parents that bad?" I couldn't help but ask even though a deep knot formed in my stomach as I anticipated what he was going to say.

"Now they aren't. Now I feel like they put in more effort to talk to me and see me than ever before. I often wonder if they're just trying to make up for their guilty consciences."

"I'm sure that's not true." I took his hand into my lap and held it between both of mine, rubbing my thumb over his palm.

"Before the accident, I barely saw them. Neither of us did. We heard them more than saw them. It seemed as though they were so hell-bent on screaming at each other whenever they got the chance that they barely remembered we even existed. It was only after the accident, and after they separated that my being their son seemed important to them."

"I'm so sorry," was all I could think to say. My heart tugged with sadness for Liam and I watched as he shrugged the weight from his shoulders and let his eyebrows soften. He brought my hand to his lips and delicately placed a kiss on my knuckles.

"What is it about you that makes it so easy for me to talk to you, to tell you things I haven't told anyone else?"

I couldn't bring myself to speak, the joy that question filled me with fought with the guilt at my own secret. Liam shifted his body closer to mine and slid his lips from my hand to my mouth, releasing my grip and instead lifting my face towards him.

Allowing myself to once again ignore the guilt that filled my lungs, I tasted his lips and embraced his hands on me. The longer I waited the more my feelings were growing and the harder it would be for me to tell Liam the truth.

After a beautiful morning walk through farmers' fields while the sun beat down on us, we had circled back around and Liam had offered for me to go back to his house for a cold drink. His mum's house was on the same side of town as mine but about another ten minutes walk past mine.

Curiosity overtook me and I needed to see the house where both Liam and Jeremy had grown up. Liam had explained to me how his mum had kept the house after the divorce and his bedroom had remained available for him when he returned home from university.

"She even kept Jeremy's room the same, as if he might come back some day," Liam told me as we settled onto the sofa with our drinks. "All his things are in boxes in his room. That's as far as anyone could convince mum to clear it out. They are all labeled ready to go to charity or the homeless."

It hit me again how horribly the accident had affected so many lives. I tried to imagine having to be the person responsible for packing and removing all of Jeremy's belongings, all the things that made him the person he was, I could barely hold it together just from the thought of it. I didn't want to know that all of Jeremy's things were still in the house. I wanted to enjoy my time with Liam, but instead, now all I could think about was Jeremy.

Later, I excused myself from the living room where Liam and I had been watching a film with Liam's arm rested comfortably over my shoulders, under the ruse of using the bathroom. After Liam told me Jeremy's things were still in his room, I felt an overwhelming urge to see it, as if I might get some sort of closure from knowing he was really gone and his things were packed away.

Looking at four doors at the top of the stairs I realised I didn't know which one belonged to Jeremy. I couldn't look through every room until I found it, Liam would notice my absence soon enough.

Three doors had been left open just a crack and one door remained firmly closed. I took a guess that the closed door was hiding the haunting memories of Jeremy's life and I tiptoed over to it.

My heart thumped strongly in my chest as my hand took its place on the cold metal door handle, slowly turning it and softly pushing the door open. It only creaked a little bit and I didn't think it would be loud enough for Liam to have heard.

My eyes were drawn to the wooden bed with a mattress with no sheets or bedding under the window. Next to that was a small wooden table holding a blue lamp and a pile of weights of various different sizes lay neatly at the foot of the bed. On the opposite side of the room was a hard wood wardrobe, with the double doors closed. Liam hadn't been lying about the boxes. There were piles of them pushed against the back wall, I could just about make out the labels stuck onto a few.

The air was stale in Jeremy's room and I guessed that no one had been in there for a while and probably no one had moved anything in there for a long time. An odd feeling came over me as my eyes scanned over what was left of Jeremy's bedroom, what was left of Jeremy's life, and my eyes began to blur with the tears that were forming.

It was almost as though Jeremy's life had been preserved in a pile of tatty cardboard boxes in the bedroom where he would have spent most of his time.

Suddenly, I was overcome fatigue and had to crouch down to stop myself from falling over. The nightmares were getting to me more now, and I wondered if I should tell Liam the truth. Maybe if he knew everything he could go to Jeremy, and my nightmares would be over. I was sure he was the answer to Jeremy moving on.

I heard Liam getting off the sofa and quickly wiped the tear that had fallen down my cheek. "Which door is the bathroom again?" I called down the stairs as I stood slowly and once again closed Jeremy's bedroom door.

-

"Have you ever been in love?" I asked Liam later that afternoon as I lay in bed next to him. His bedroom was so bare I wondered if he had ever actually lived in that house at all. His suit case was open on the floor with clothes skewed around it, a dark chest of drawers leant against the wall opposite the bed and a simple desk and chair were the only other furniture in the room.

"Where did that question come from?" he asked as he slid his head over to watch me with his beautiful flecked eyes.

I met his gaze. "I just want to get to know you some more. You've met my ex; I just want to know about yours."

Liam sighed and sat up. "I thought I might have been last year. But the relationship ended before it came to that."

My eyes scanned his back, and I allowed my hand to slide over his skin. "What happened?"

"I wanted a relationship and she didn't," Liam confessed without turning back to meet my eyes.

"And other than that, have you had any relationships?" I asked, curiosity taking over me.

"Nothing worth mentioning." Liam turned his head to me and dropped his body again until his face was only a few centimeters from mine. I bit my lip as his beautiful eyes searched mine. "I'd like to get to know you better in a different way," he said.

I laughed and wrapped my arms happily around his neck. For a moment I was able to forget my nightmares and just enjoy what was in front of me.

# Chapter 27

I lay wide awake in bed that night, staring aimlessly at the white ceiling. Thoughts of Liam's lips filled my active mind, the feeling of his warm strong hands on my body remained imprinted on my skin. When I had first spotted Liam in the café in town, I had no idea that I might develop such feelings for him or that I might continue spending time with him after that first meeting.

I thought of Jeremy and the danger awaiting me if I reentered the forest. Although I still spent every night with Jeremy while I slept, when I awoke it was like it was all a distant memory. I could barely get a clear picture of him in my mind.

Desperately, I tried to remember the good times I had spent at the park with Jeremy playing games and eating sweets, but I realised that I could barely recall all the activities we had done together. It was only less than a week ago that I had last visited him but already it was fading enough to make me wonder if it had ever really happened.

Perhaps it was all in my imagination. Perhaps I didn't really need to tell Jeremy anything.

When I finally drifted to sleep, I found Jeremy waiting for me. I had gotten used to him begging me to come back, to stay with him. His mood could swing from desperation to anger in mere minutes. I knew in my dream state he couldn't get to me; he couldn't hurt me. What I hadn't expected was to see tears staining his cheeks.

"You came back then?" he said, wiping his nose with the back of his hand. Nothing surrounded us, just the shadows of the trees.

"Yes," I said gently. "You bring me back every night. I don't choose to be here."

"You're forgetting about me. I can feel it." The tears in his eyes made the blue look even more like the ocean.

"I don't even know if you're real," I told him honestly. I knew I should be angrier, but I had been taken by surprise seeing him so sad.

"Come back to the park, Mae. You'll see I'm real." Lights began to come into my vision as the park came into view around us. Jeremy was sat on the floor by the sweet booth. Mrs. Millar appeared, staring down her nose at me, as usual. Her head was slowly shaking side to side.

"You know I can't."

His eyes dried up instantly and I took a step away from his rising figure. He let out a breath, his nostrils blaring.

"Mae," he said, stepping towards me while I took another step back. "You will come back for me. I know you will."

"No," I said again.

Suddenly, Jeremy dived forward, his wild eyes locking onto mine, as his strong hands took hold of my arms, squeezing them so tightly I couldn't deny the pain. He hadn't touched me in a dream before and I'd thought he wouldn't be able to. Jeremy pulled me so close to him I could feel his breath on my cheek where I turned my face away from him.

"If you won't come here, maybe I'll have to find a way to come to you," he said to my turned head.

Sweat drenched my bed when I woke up that morning, and my arms ached. I could still smell his sweet breath, and when I lifted my arm, I noticed finger shaped bruises on my skin. My heart pounded as I realised he had touched me through my dream. I wasn't safe from him anywhere.

I pulled my duvet up to my chin like a shield. I knew I had to do something about him, and I had to do it now. I was no longer safe from him. What if he could leave the park? What would he do to me?

Grabbing my phone immediately I texted Liam. I had to tell him the truth as soon as I could and find a way to get him to help me. I couldn't take it any longer.

The sun had only just risen and I didn't expect a reply any time soon, most normal people didn't tend to wake up early when they didn't have to.

I started my day with a large mug of coffee, adding only a small drop of semi skimmed milk, and having a quick chat with my mum before taking what was left of my drink upstairs to my bedroom to drink as I tried to decide the best way to dress myself for the day ahead. There was a good chance if I told Liam the truth he would never want to see me again. This would be the last outfit he saw me in.

I left my curtains firmly closed, only peeking out quickly to check that there was no one spying at my window, and no new shadows in our garden, or the neighbors, that shouldn't be there.

I applied my makeup with the help of the creamy light bulb hanging from the ceiling.

A message came through on my phone and I dove onto my bed to see what it said, leaving only one eye fully surrounded with makeup and one completely bare.

"Are you free around 2 this afternoon?"

I had hoped he would want to meet up earlier in the day, perhaps for breakfast or coffee, so I could get the job done quickly, before Jeremy had the chance to find me. Instead, it seemed I would be waiting around for him most of the day.

I replied to let him know that was fine and I would meet him at two pm.

I went back down stairs to sit in the comfort of my mum's presence. When I got downstairs, she was picking up her keys and pulling her handbag over her shoulder.

"Are you going out?" I asked, a little desperately. My heart began to speed up again.

"I have work," she said. "Dad is already at work so you'll have the house to yourself until dinner."

"Oh... Okay." I would have felt a lot more comfortable with someone else here to witness if Jeremy came for me and dragged me away.

"Mae, are you okay?" mum asked. "You're white as a sheet."

"Fine," I assured her, with a fake smile. "Just need to get out in the sun today."

When my mum was far enough away from the house not to notice, I locked the door and closed all the curtains.

In Liam's next message he offered to meet me at my house and said we could decide what to do together from there. I supposed with both my parents both working that afternoon my house would be as good as any place to have a serious conversation. At least it would be private.

Unable to focus on any one thing that day while I waited for Liam to arrive, I spent most of my time wandering aimlessly round the empty house, tweaking already straight photo frames and plumping cushions that were already in perfect shape. I washed up every plate and utensil I dirtied as soon as I was done with it just for something to distract me from obsessively checking the locks and peering around the curtains every time someone walked by the house.

Over and over again I rehearsed what I would say to Liam when he arrived, and rehearsed how I would react when he didn't believe me, deciding how best to convince him I was being honest.

When two pm finally arrived, I found myself leaning against the front window watching down the street for when Liam would turn round the corner and make his way to the front door of my house. As soon as I spotted his figure I ran to the door and waited with my hand already on the door handle.

A knock came on the door and I jumped, having expected him to ring the bell. I took a breath so as to not seem like I had been waiting behind the door for him and then opened it with a broad smile pasted over my face. "Hi!" Liam smiled back, oblivious to what was to come. He placed a deliciously warm kiss on my lips and I tried not to let the sadness of what I had to do show on my face. I invited him inside and took him straight through to the kitchen where I seated him at the wooden dining table.

"How are you?" I asked, as I poured us both a glass of lemonade with ice. Liam's red cheeks suggested the day was as hot as it looked. I hadn't been able to bring myself to go outside while I had waited. I had watched the beautiful weather from the cool interior of the house.

"Good thanks," Liam replied, taking the cold drink from me. "Sorry I couldn't meet this morning; mum was finally getting rid of dad's old stuff that she packed into the garage when he left. Needless to say, there were a lot of dump trips." Liam plonked himself down in the chair nearest the door. I nodded in response but my mouth remained closed. "I tried to talk about doing Jeremy's things as well, but it was a little much for one day."

I sat in the chair opposite him, still not saying anything.

"Are you okay?" Liam's hand found its way to mine and I squeezed it gently before removing it from my grasp. I knew he wouldn't want to hold my hand when he knew what I had to say, but I didn't think I would be able to handle the rejection if he took his hand away first.

"Look, I wanted to talk to you about something actually," I said, lowering my face, barely able to look in his eyes. I knew I had to get right to the point or I would lose my nerve again.

Liam's face fell a little and then he lifted his eyebrows with concern. "Is everything okay?"

I took a deep breath and looked up to meet his gaze in order to make sure he knew I was being serious. "This is going to sound really strange, just hear me out, okay?" I started, nervously. "So, a couple weeks ago... I met... I met Jeremy."

Liam's face creased with confusion and I could tell it would take quite some explaining for him to understand.

"Well not really him. I met his spirit." I had forgotten everything I had spent all day rehearsing and everything I said seemed to be coming out in a jumble. "I was in the woods at that old abandoned amusement park, you know the one? Well of course you do, sorry. Anyway, well, Jeremy was there, he led me to this other amusement park, one that was still working. Or at least I thought it was. It turned out not to be real, he made it with his mind, and he's stuck there now. His spirit I mean. Well, not just his spirit, he has a physical form but he isn't really there."

A blank expression took over Liam's face as I spoke and I wondered if he was even listening to what I was saying. I continued anyway, afraid that if I stopped there I wouldn't start again. Even as I spoke, I felt the clear memories of Jeremy slipping into darkness as if I had imagined the whole thing.

"And anyway, as I said he is a spirit and he's stuck so the only way for him to move onto the afterlife, and probably heaven, is if you come with me to his park. I think he needs to see you again to move on."

When I'd finished, I let out a long breath and waited for Liam's response. When he hadn't replied after a few moments, and his expressionless face hadn't changed, I said his name.

He started to nod slowly and his eyes squinted until finally he spoke. "Is this supposed to be a joke? This isn't funny, Mae."

"No, Liam, I'm not joking, you have to believe me," I begged him. I couldn't start to understand what he might be feeling at that moment, or what he could be thinking of me, but I knew I had to continue.

Liam's eyes wandered the room for a while, clearly deep in thought. "So, when we met, you said you knew Jeremy. Was that a lie?" he asked, surprisingly calmly.

"Yes. I mean, I did know him by then but I had only just met him, I didn't know him while he was alive."

Liam's slow nodding turned into him shaking his head in denial. "Why are you doing this? What do you want from me?"

"I just need you to come with me to see Jeremy… To help him move on."

Slamming his chair backwards so that it clattered onto the floor of the kitchen, Liam stood up quickly and looked straight into my eyes. His voice took on a much louder, angrier tone as he spoke next. "What the fuck, Mae? What kind of sick joke are you trying to pull? I thought we were friends, more than friends. Were you using me this whole time? Why?"

Fire burned in Liam's eyes and his sudden outburst surprised me enough to lose my words. I said the only thing I could think of. "Please, believe me, Liam."

Without another word Liam left the kitchen in a storm of confused furious energy and I heard the front door slam behind him as he went, leaving me in a final disappointing silence.

Moments passed while I did nothing but stare at the wooden chair which lay helplessly on the kitchen floor, my mind racing as I went through everything I had said to Liam, and what I could have said or done differently. Was there any scenario where he would actually believe me? No, the only way Liam would believe me was if he saw Jeremy with his own eyes, I thought to myself.

The betrayal that had been pasted across Liam's face shot through my heart as I thought of the pain, I must have just caused him. I thought of it from his perspective, this girl he had just met and possibly was beginning to have real feelings for had come out with such unreasonable nonsense about his dead brother, the death that he had spent years trying to recover from. I couldn't imagine how hurt he must feel.

Burning hot tears began to crowd my eyes and I allowed one to run down my cheek as I thought of what a mistake I had made. I should never have told Liam; I should have just forgotten Jeremy entirely and moved on with my life. But he wouldn't allow that.

Another tear edged its way from my eye and over my cheeks, as the thought of abandoning Jeremy to live for eternity by himself took hold of my brain. Before I knew it more and more hot tears scorched my cheeks, until barely any of the makeup I had spent so long perfecting remained around my eyes and instead was running awkwardly over my face.

I sobbed into my hands as I let the reality of my situation sink in, gulping air into my lungs whenever I could manage. Everything had gone so wrong. Meeting Jeremy had seemed amazing at first, like a gift to me after being so distraught about the end of my relationship with George, but that had all shattered when I found out he was dead.

Meeting Liam was never meant to turn into the beautiful relationship it had become, I'd had no intentions of growing such deep feelings for this man, but the more time I spent with him the more I realised what a lovely, caring soul he had, what a generous and thoughtful man he would be.

It had never been my intentions to ignore my friends and make them worry about me while I was off kissing a boy that I couldn't even introduce to them.

Most of all, I had never intended to cause the pain I had witnessed in Liam's eyes, his beautiful eyes. This man I had come to care deeply about, and knew how much he had already had to deal with in his life. Knowing that the relationship we had been forming was now over so quickly, was enough to make my body feel weak and my heart hurt.

When the tears finally stopped and exhaustion took over me, I sat for a long time at the kitchen table and contemplated all the decisions I had made and what I could possibly do next. I wanted to call Liam, to explain to him that I was telling the truth, to beg him to believe me, but I knew he wouldn't believe me, even if by some miracle he did answer my call, which I doubted very much.

By the time my parents were both due home from work I had retrieved the chair from the kitchen floor and placed it neatly under the table, and was just washing off the remaining bit of makeup from under my eyes.

It was one of those rare nights where both my parents were off work at the same time. Usually on those sorts of evenings they preferred we all ate dinner as a family if I was also home, but that day I was struggling to find the enthusiasm to socialise and pretend like everything was fine.

When the time came that my mum's gentle voice beckoned me down for dinner, I took a deep breath and forced a smile to stretch across my face. I could tell that my fake happiness wasn't quite making it to my eyes but I told myself I would just keep them pointed at my food.

Dad was dishing up when I made my way into the kitchen, I offered to help but as it was only soup and the table was already set, he told me to take my seat. He placed a bowl of homemade creamy leek and potato soup in front of each of us and then took his seat opposite my mum, the seat Liam had been sitting in only a few hours before. I wondered what Liam was having for dinner.

Taking only a few bites of the fresh roll dad had provided and sipping slowly at each spoon full of soup my parents soon noticed I was not myself.

"Everything okay?" Dad asked.

"Fine, just tired today I think."

"Long day of laying in the sun again?" Dad laughed.

I smirked. "Jealous you decided to work before starting university rather than relax?"

"I can't imagine anything worse than spending months sitting around on my bum all day." Dad had always sworn by after school, weekend and holiday jobs for teenagers. He had very much encouraged me to get mine in the first place and hadn't been best pleased when I hadn't looked for a new one when the business went under, deciding to spend my last summer before university relaxing and enjoying my time. If I had known how my summer would go, I may have chosen to stay in work instead.

"Well, you know I plan to get a job as soon as I get to Lincoln," I told him seriously. I wanted my parents to know that I was not going to university to waste the next few years of my life. I didn't mention that although I did plan on taking my courses seriously, I also planned to take part in the socialising part of the university experience, and if a party or two should go along with that I wouldn't be complaining.

"Are you feeling ready then?" Mum asked. "Got everything ready for university?"

"Mostly, I'll need to get some toiletries and that stuff but I'm sure I can get that when I get there so there's less to transfer," I told them. I'd had all my household items bought and ready for months, some of it my parents had purchased for me when they could, trying desperately to be a part of the next stage of my life.

"I'm sure we can fit it all in the car if there is anything else you need," Mum said reasonably.

"Thank you," I said to both my parents.

After dinner I filled the dishwasher up then sat on the sofa beside my parents. Before long I decided that wasn't the way to stop myself from thinking about Liam or Jeremy and the regrets I was having at that moment.

I quickly sent Jayne a text to see if she wanted to hang out and then assuming she would say yes, I started getting my shoes ready and located a jacket to wear when the sun had gone down fully and the chill was setting in.

As I said "goodbye" to my parents and went to open the front door my mum called after me. "What time will you be home?"

"Ten at the latest," I said remembering her new house rules.

Jayne's reply didn't come through until I was already wandering slowly in the direction of her house.

"We're all at George's. His parents aren't home so walk straight in when you get here."

As if hanging out at my ex-boyfriend's house was really what I wanted to be doing.

"Have you told the guys I'm coming?" I replied.

"Yes," Jayne's next message said. I couldn't now come up with an excuse as to why I couldn't make it, especially as I was the one to send the first message.

As much as I tried to convince myself that it wouldn't be weird or awkward, I still couldn't persuade my legs to move with any speed. The bare

214

skin on my face was blanketed with the early evening warmth, and a golden hue was beginning to stream through the sky. A few people were still around on the streets, making their way out to dinner or only just making their way home from work.

For a moment I thought I saw Liam walking ahead of me and my heart began to race as I tried to quickly decide if it would be better to give him his space and not tell him I was there or to call his name and hope that he had forgiven me and may even believe me now. Before I could make the decision, the man turned the corner and I saw his face was half covered in a dark beard which did not belong to Liam. Fiercely swallowing the lump that had risen into my throat I continued walking with my head down.

The walk to George's house was almost the same as to Jayne's, he lived only one street over and his house was almost identical, much like I imagined all the other houses in the estate must have been.

My hand hesitated as it hovered over the long silver door handle, deciding whether or not to open the door. The window above the door was ajar and I could hear all my friends' voices floating out, they were laughing at something and I longed to be a part of the fun again. As much as I wanted to be included, I knew that as soon as I entered everyone would go quiet and an awkward air would fill the room.

I let out the breath I had been holding tightly in my chest and pushed the handle down, letting myself quietly into the house.

"Mae," Jayne's voice called. "We are in the bedroom."

"Okay, just taking my shoes off," I called back, forcing a cheerful tone into my voice. I made my way up the carpeted stairs to the only room with the door closed most of the way.

"Hi," I said as I entered the room. I hadn't been back in Geroge's room since we had broken up and it looked exactly as it had the last time I'd seen it. George lay on the floor leant up against the side of the bed, PlayStation controller in his hands; Adam sat in an almost identical position with an identical controller in his hands. Neither of them looked my way as I walked in, they both grunted a quick "hello" while they continued to battle on whatever game it was they played.

At the top of the bed, on the blue checkered duvet, Jayne held Tommy's thick arm around her shoulder and leant her head against his shoulder. She lifted her head briefly to greet me as I joined them on the bed, sitting on the opposite end, and then replaced it.

"How's it going?" I asked everyone collectively.

"Bit boring honestly," Jayne said. "Been watching the guys play games all afternoon."

"Have they let you have a go this time at least?" I asked, trying to start the evening on a lighter note.

"No, guess they can't get over how good I was last time," Jayne smirked.

"You mean when you lost and almost broke the controller by throwing it at the wall," George scoffed from his seat on the floor. From where he sat I could see the back of his head and just barely the very side of his face. Remembering when I used to slide my fingers through his soft, dark hair I wondered if it would feel the same now.

I lifted my eyes from the back of George's head to see Jayne's eyes glued to mine. I lowered my eyes into my lap and avoided her curious stare.

"So, why haven't we seen you much recently? I thought when you broke it off with that Jeremy guy we would be seeing you more," Jayne said, accusingly.

I looked at my lap. "I've just been busy I guess."

"Right," Jayne said, unconvinced. I could feel her eyes still studying my face. "Wait. You aren't seeing someone else are you?"

"Well-"

"Oh my god! Mae!" Jayne exclaimed. "You've been bailing on us for a guy. Again!"

"I didn't mean to bail on you!" I insisted. "I just didn't want you to think badly of me seeing someone else already. And I didn't know if it would last."

"Has it lasted? Are you still with him?"

"I guess." I couldn't exactly tell them that we had broken up. I wasn't totally sure we had.

"Well, go on then. Tell us about him." All the men in the group had been silent so far through the conversation, and I couldn't help glancing at George again. "Oh, don't worry about them. They aren't listening to our girl chat anyway."

I searched my mind for something I could say about him in front of my ex-boyfriend.

"Well like I said it's really new, and I don't know if it'll work out."

Jayne rolled her eyes and shook her head. "Don't be silly, even if nothing comes of it, I still want to know."

"He's really funny," I said, trying not to make it obvious how much I had begun to like him. I didn't want Jayne to think I would fall for any and every guy that looked my way. I told her casually about Liam being an older man and how he went to university.

"Ooo an older man." She wiggled her hips in excitement.

I was embarrassed to be talking about another guy after not long ago getting excited about Jeremy. I didn't mention to Jayne or anyone else that Liam was Jeremy's brother or that Liam's brother has died a few years earlier.

"Have you seen Liam today then?" Jayne asked loudly.

"Yes, just for a little while," I told her honestly, giving no other details. Even though I could finally say I felt completely over George and our relationship, I still felt weird discussing a possible new boyfriend in his presence.

"You should have brought him tonight so we could all meet him!" Jayne suddenly sat up straight with what she thought was a brilliant idea.

"Maybe next time," I said awkwardly.

"Why don't you call him now?" Jayne said, expectantly.

"I... He's busy tonight," I said, stuttering to find a reason why I couldn't call him. Even if I did call him, I doubted he would answer.

"What could he be doing that he couldn't drop for you?" she pouted. The three guys in the room remained very quiet and all had their heads turned stiffly at the TV.

I searched my mind for an answer that would satisfy her. "He's helping his mum with some house stuff."

Jayne sighed loudly but seemed to accept that answer. No one said anything for a while and I searched my mind for a conversation starter that would fit the group and take the focus off me and more specifically off Liam. Just as a few ideas began to form in my mind Tommy spoke.

"I don't remember a Liam in our year," he said curiously. "Did he go to the same sixth form as us?"

As I opened my mouth Jayne answered for me. "No, Mae just said, he's a bit older"

Tommy's eyes met mine over Jayne's head and he raised his eyebrows in the way he did when Jayne spoke over him, which she often did. I smirked in reply, and then nodded in agreement.

"How did you meet him if not at school?" Adam chimed in without turning his face away from the game.

As it turned out they were all listening to our "girl talk".

"I met him at one of the cafes in town," I explained, leaving out the messages we shared before meeting in person. "We were both getting coffee and I supposed we just started talking."

I could see the back of Adam's head nod in understanding, or perhaps it was more to pretend he understood when really he had forgotten to listen to my response, too preoccupied with winning his game against George.

Although this wasn't the subject of conversation I had hoped for that evening, I was glad to be talking like a group again, and after the last couple of weeks I felt I was ready to truly relax and allow myself to spend time with my friends again. If only I could finish the small job of getting Jeremy's spirit to move on then I could officially start my summer of relaxation and fun. "Would we know him?" Tommy asked. "What's his last name?"

"Brown," I said hesitantly.

"Of course," Jayne said, instantly taking out her phone. "I can't believe I didn't think to find him online before."

My fingers and toes were tingling with my sudden increased heartbeat.

"You don't have to do that," I croaked.

George hadn't said a word since the subject of Liam had come up and I was somehow relieved he wasn't getting involved.

"Wait, I think I know who he is." Jayne continued to type into her phone and scroll through her findings before filling us in on her discovery. "Do you guys remember when we went to that old amusement park a few weeks ago that had closed down because someone died?" My pulse was racing furiously by that point. "Well, this is his brother. Liam's brother is the guy that died at the amusement park."

All four of my friends turned their heads towards me, even George briefly removed his eyes from where they had been glued to the TV since I had arrived.

"Did you know?" Adam asked curiously.

I shook my head slowly taking a long gulp. "He never mentioned it." I wasn't sure why I'd lied. He had mentioned it and even if that wasn't the reason we had met in the first place I was sure it would have come up between us by now.

"That's so sad," Jayne whispered. I didn't say anything else on the matter and clearly no one else knew what to say either as we all sat in a morbid silence for a long time, until finally George started their game up again.

Thankfully the conversation soon moved on to a topic that had nothing to do with me, Liam or Jeremy, and not only could I join in on the discuss but also George joined in, and on occasion we were able to reply to each other, and things started to feel normal again, as normal as they possibly could. I even found myself laughing on occasion, something which seemed almost alien to me with this group at that point.

When it came time for me to start walking home, I found that I was actually a little disappointed to be leaving. Adam had left an hour earlier claiming he still needed to have dinner but Tommy and Jayne didn't seem in any rush. I showed myself out into the fresh evening air, sliding my thin denim jacket over my arms and onto my shoulders as I closed the door behind myself.

The silence of the night wrapped itself around me and with nothing to occupy my mind I found that I could do nothing else but recall the conversation I'd had with Liam earlier that day, picturing exactly how he had reacted and the sadness that had filled his eyes before the rage had set in.

I took out my phone and slowly allowed my legs to carry me home while I wrote out a message to Liam. I went over it again and again until I finally decided to send it before I backed out.

"Liam, I'm so sorry for earlier, but I need you to believe me. I know I sound like a lunatic and trust me I have been wondering about my sanity since this all began, but I really am telling the truth. Please believe me and I will prove it to you. Please."

I pressed send just as I made it to the front door of my house. I didn't want to put my phone away after that, I wanted to watch the screen as I waited for a reply, but I knew the likelihood of receiving any sort of reply from Liam was quite unlikely, so I put my phone back into my pocket and walked into the house.

"You're early," my mum's cheery voice called from where she and my dad were still curled up in front of the TV.

I glanced at the clock on the wall before replying. "I'm not sure two minutes to ten counts as early."

"It's not late so I'm taking that as a win," Mum grinned.

"I'll give you that one." I smiled back, taking a seat next to her on the sofa. I didn't recognise the film they were watching, it looked old, like it might have been made in the 90s.

"Did you have a good time with your friends?" Dad asked.

Just as I went to reply I felt my phone vibrate in my pocket and a shot of anticipation burst through my body. "It was good, thanks. I'm actually pretty tired now, so I think I'm going to go to bed," I said, quickly excusing myself and running upstairs to read his reply from the privacy of my bedroom.

Grabbing my phone out of my pocket as soon as the door had closed behind me, I saw Jayne's name appear on the screen. Disappointment deflated me and I collapsed on top of my bed, not bothering to look at the message. I'll never hear from him again, I thought to myself in defeat.

When eventually I allowed myself out of my depressed slump, I turned my phone off, accepting that if Liam decided to reply it wouldn't be tonight, and I didn't want to keep getting my hopes up every time I got a notification on my phone.

My tired eyes remained wide open for most of the night, mostly because images of Liam's betrayed face flashed before me whenever I closed them, but also with the memories of Jeremy's hands on me while I slept the night before. I couldn't allow myself to take the chance of him getting a hold of me again.

# Chapter 29

When sleep finally took me Jeremy haunted my dreams, teasing my inability to help him. He laughed at me through the bars of the cage I found myself in once again, and I cowered from him, holding my hands in front of my body stopping him from coming for me. Suddenly his face grew sad and his eyes faded to the colour of a rainy sky. "I'm sorry, Mae," dream Jeremy said and suddenly I was standing in front of him, the bars of the cage had disappeared as I wrapped my arms around his shoulders and allowed his head to rest on my shoulder as Jeremy cried. "It's going to be okay," I told him before the dream faded away and my eyes snapped open.

Confusion filled my tired mind as my eyes watched the dust floating in the sun rays that had somehow found their way through the gaps in my curtains.

Outside my bedroom door I could hear my parents moving around, in and out of the bathroom and then making their way softly downstairs where the kettle was soon boiling. Their voices floated through the ceiling into my bedroom and I wondered what they were talking about so early in the morning. Soon I could hear their coffee cups and cereal bowls being put in the dishwasher before their footsteps took them out of the kitchen and into the hallway by the front door. The whispered voices went quiet and heard the front door open and close as they both left the house and started their separate journeys to work.

It had been two nights since Jeremy threatened to leave the park and come for me, but I had yet to see any evidence of his escape. The waiting seemed to be worse than I could imagine his presence in my real life would be. Could there really be a way for him to leave the park?

I couldn't spend another day by myself in the empty house, jumping at every noise.

After breakfast I pulled on my shoes and left the house, not entirely sure where I was going. My mind was so preoccupied thinking about both Brown brothers I didn't even notice myself wander over the entrance to the woodland that led to the abandoned amusement park. Once I noticed where I was headed, I wanted to turn back, but I couldn't.

I sluggishly stepped over fallen branches and encroaching leaves. It was if the path had closed up in the short time that I hadn't been using it. I didn't know why I was even walking that way. I couldn't access the park during the day, which I was sure meant Jeremy wouldn't be able to leave during the day either. But his threat to come after me remained at the front of my mind.

When I arrived at the abandoned amusement park, I took a few minutes to take it in again; the memory of a very different time remained in the old and broken equipment.

The birds were the only noise I could hear from there, and the occasional shuffle of the leaves in the trees. I was surprised more people didn't know about this place; it was perfect for teenagers to meet up without the watchful eyes of authority. I supposed it had been long enough since the accident that it had been mostly forgotten about.

I sauntered over to the broken wall that signified the entrance to Jeremy's Amusement Park and leant against the hard stone as my eyes took in the darkness between the trees. I felt almost relieved to look into at the empty forest instead of the flashing lights of the park.

As I was beginning to feel quite relaxed the light of two, bright, blue eyes flashed through the shadows of the trees.

The shock straightened my spine and I did the only thing I could think of. I ran.

I ran away from the eyes watching me from the woodland, and didn't look back until I'd made it home. I locked the door behind me and leant against it, heaving for breath. Although sweat covered my body I felt cold all over.

My arms wrapped tightly round my body and I sat against the front door until I had retrieved my breath. My heart beat didn't slow quite to its normal rhythm but it was enough to get off the floor.

Did I really see them? I asked myself. Or was it my anxieties creating things that weren't there? I had barely slept the night before or for many nights before that. Perhaps they weren't really there.

But what if they were there? What did that mean? Was Jeremy watching me? Was he waiting for me?

Alone again in the house, I sat in silence for the rest of the day, holding my legs to my chest, listening for anyone approaching.

"Why is the door locked?" Dad asked, when he arrived home.

"I must've just done it automatically," I lied.

I wouldn't let myself sleep that night. Every time I felt myself drifting, I would force myself awake with a jolt. I must have drifted asleep at some point early in the morning though because I opened my eyes to the sun pouring through my window.

Loneliness seemed to settle over me as I knew I was once again by myself in the house. In the past it was rare that I wished my parents were home, to keep me company, but with the threat of Jeremy on my mind, I was left with an uncertain feeling in the pit of my stomach and the thought of dealing with it by myself only made me feel that much more unsettled.

A knocking came from the front door as I was pulling the duvet over my head again, and I knew it had to be him. It was Jeremy, finally coming for me. I couldn't put him off forever, but perhaps with the door locked I would be safe inside.

When the knocking came again, louder and faster than the first time, I decided to give in to my fate.

Quickly pulling on a hoodie and a pair of shorts, I slouched downstairs to answer the door. It wasn't Jeremy I discovered on my door step.

Liam's face seemed to be as confused as mine when I opened the door, revealing him on the doorstep. He looked freshly showered, his hair was still a little damp, his hands were stuffed into the pockets of his jeans and he wore a plain blue t-shirt with no jacket.

"Were you in bed," he said, his tone wasn't unkind but he didn't appear happy to see me, in fact the more I stared at him I began to see that he didn't look happy at all. Dark circles lay under his eyes and his normally tall back was hunched forward.

"Yes." Only then, with Liam's eyes searching my face, did I realise that I had not even bothered to wash my face or at least run my fingers through my hair before opening the door to him. Liam nodded and then let his eyes drop from my face and his gaze landed on the floor between us. "Why are you here?"

He let out a deep breath before speaking again. "I think we should talk."

This was all I had hoped for, for Liam to talk to me again, but now he had said it I didn't know what to say, or do for that matter. I hadn't even expected Liam to reply to my text let alone find him on my doorstep at eight in the morning.

"Can I come in?" he said at last. "Or should we go somewhere else?"

"No," I said quickly, gladly holding the door open for him. "Come in."

I told him to take a seat in the living room and then I ran upstairs to see what I could do about making myself presentable. I washed my face and brushed my teeth, and without time for a shower I sprayed some deodorant under my arms. Lastly, before joining Liam I pulled a brush through my hair, one thing I had noticed since cutting my hair short was that it was much more noticeable when tufts were standing out at odd angles. Liam was sitting with his chin in his hands and his elbows rested on top of his knees when I reentered the living room. Worrying that he might move away from me if I sat too close to him on the sofa, I made myself comfortable on the rarely used armchair by the window.

I held my breath as I waited for Liam, who appeared to be deep in thought, to talk first.

"First of all," Liam finally said seriously. "I just want to say that yes you do sound like a lunatic, and I don't know what to think of all this. But I just need to know."

His eyes remained firmly pointed at the coffee table as he spoke and I tried to ignore the shooting pain that I felt when he called me a "lunatic". I couldn't blame him for thinking that, I knew how it sounded.

"What would you like to know?" I said gently.

"Everything," Liam said, his emerald eyes finally meeting mine. "I want to know every detail from the moment you met him until now. What did he say? Where was he? What did he do? Just tell me everything."

Without hesitation I did what he said and started to tell him the whole long story of going to the old amusement park with my friends, seeing Jeremy and having him lead me to his own park. I told Liam how we had played the games and went on the rides, I told him about Mrs. Millar and all the other people I saw again every time I visited. I explained how Jeremy had captured me to prevent me from leaving him. The only details I left out were those that might suggest there had been anything more than friendship between us. Although, as I was all too aware these days, Jeremy had never felt the same way I had.

Liam sat, listening with no emotion or reactions on display. It was only when I mentioned the cage that his eyebrows rose ever so slightly, and then returned to their original position so quickly I thought I might have imagined it.

We sat in silence again when I finished speaking, I held my hands in my lap to stop them from shaking. Part of me was waiting for Liam to react again like he had the day before, storming out of the house in disbelief.

"So," Liam finally said. "If Jeremy is really there, and he doesn't want to move on to the afterlife, as you said, why bother telling me at all? Why not just leave him?"

I kept my voice light as I replied. "He's dead, Liam. He needs to go to heaven." Liam didn't say anything so I expanded on my answer. "Besides, he won't leave me alone. He's able to talk to me every time I sleep. I'm not getting any rest. I can't go on like this."

"And you can only see him at night?" Liam asked.

"Yes."

"Tonight then," Liam said, looking at me.

"What?"

"Take me to him tonight, so I can finally know once and for all if you're right, mad, or for some twisted reason just messing with me."

"Tonight?" I confirmed.

"I'll meet you here at eleven," Liam said standing up and heading to the door.

"That's it then?" I said, desperate to hang out with him, talk to him, laugh with him. "You're just leaving?"

"Mae, until I know what's really going on, I just can't be with you." The way he said my name was enough to break me, and with the rest of his confession I could barely breathe. I nodded in reply, of course he was right. How could we go back to the way we were the first few days we had hung out when we were waiting to find out whether or not Liam could see his dead brother again?

"Wait," I called as he left. "Don't knock on the door later. I'll meet you down the street. My parents can't know."

Liam nodded in reply then turned his broad back in my direction. I watched him walk away for only a moment before closing the door and locking it.

# Chapter 30

That day passed in a haze of nerves and overthinking. With the plans now set I began to wonder if I had imagined it all. I feared that we would arrive at the abandoned amusement park and then I would lead Liam into the woods to find nothing but trees. What would he think of me? I wondered. Then I realised it wouldn't matter what Liam felt about me if I couldn't show him the amusement park because that would prove that none of it had been real and I had imagined the whole thing.

And what if we did make it to the amusement park? What if Liam wasn't the answer?

My dad arrived home an hour earlier than my mum, and by the time she walked through the front door we were already dishing up dinner. Relief flooded her tired face as she realised she wouldn't have to cook.

After dinner she told me she had the next day off and asked if I would like to spend it with her. I had hoped that after tonight Liam would forgive me and that we would spend the next day together, getting back on track to a functioning relationship. When I saw the hope in her eyes, I realised I couldn't disappoint her. I agreed and decided Liam and I could always hang out in the evening. Sometimes I forgot that at the end of the summer I would not only be leaving the town I grew up in, I would also be leaving my parents. I was sure they thought about that fact a lot more often than I did.

I excused myself to my bedroom at ten-thirty pm expecting my parents to follow close behind. Panic gripped me when I realised they had no plans of going to bed any time soon. All my plans to escape the house without them noticing required they be tucked away in their own room, there was no route to either the front or back door that didn't involve walking past the living room where they remained very much awake.

I watched the time passing as my leg shook and I pictured Liam waiting outside, expecting to see me any minute now.

Finally, at eleven pm, my parents began to get ready for bed. After ten minutes of hearing them walking around and their whispered conversation, their door closed and quiet rolled through the house. I sent a quick text to Liam to tell him I would be coming out soon. The thought of disappointing my parents by once again sneaking out of the house in the middle of the night, only to return as the sun was rising the next morning, caused me to hesitate, but I knew I had no other choice. I couldn't wait until I knew they would definitely be asleep, I had to go soon.

I'd left my bedroom door open ever so slightly to create as little noise as possible when I slid into the hall way and down the stairs. I picked up my shoes on the way to the front door and held them under my arm.

The next noisy obstacle in my way was removing the key that had been left in the lock and preventing the six other keys on the keyring from rattling as I did so. Then I had to replace it with my own key to unlock the door. My hand shook as I placed it softly around the keys, preventing them from hitting against each other as I pulled the key out of the door, then tactically placed them on the sofa rather than the hard wooden side table.

My heart was beating in overtime, warning me to hurry up before my parents inevitably came downstairs to see what the noise was. Quickly, I used my key to unlock the door and then opened and closed it as I had practiced many times that day, locking it behind myself.

Running down the street silently to where Liam was leaning against the short wall of a neighboring driveway, I didn't allow myself to feel like my escape had been a success until I had pulled Liam's arm and taken him around the corner where my parents could not see us if they came out of the house.

"You're not wearing shoes," Liam finally said when I had decided we were safe.

I had forgotten all about the trainers I hugged tightly to my chest and slipped them onto my feet as I explained how I had been trying not to disturb my parents. Liam nodded, seemingly unfazed by the panic burning in my veins.

"How are you?" I asked, still speaking softly as if someone would hear us.

"Fine," Liam said. We set off walking and I had to hurry to keep up with Liam's long steps, whether he noticed me struggling to keep pace with him or not he didn't slow down.

Liam kept his eyes ahead and didn't look towards me once for the entire walk out of town, every time I spoke, he either ignored me or replied in short, unfriendly answers. I couldn't imagine how he must be feeling at that moment, knowing he might see his dead brother while also knowing that was impossible, but even with all that, his attitude stung.

Silence surrounded us as we walked through the woods, I had given up trying to talk to Liam and we saw no one else on our journey. Somehow the walk seemed to last a lot longer that night than it had felt any of the times I had walked it by myself.

I wondered what would happen if I couldn't find Jeremy that night, would life just return to normal, or would I start to see other dead people? The thought sent a shiver down my spine and I almost tripped on a large tree root as I tried to rid myself of worries of how mad I might really be.

My hand was suddenly enveloped by the warmth of Liam's as he caught me and stopped me from falling any further. I smiled at him and he instantly released my hand and looked away stuffing his fist into his jeans pocket. I refrained from looking at him for the rest of the walk.

# Chapter 31

Liam hesitated as he came through the trees and entered the old, rusted amusement park. Watching his dark, emerald eyes travel over each and every piece of rusted metal only to settle on the broken roller coaster, I realised suddenly that this must have been the first time he had been back since the accident.

Remaining by the forest while saying nothing I let Liam take in the sights around him. I was sure I had spotted a tear forming in his eye but just as quickly he blinked and it disappeared.

"What happens now?" he asked. The moment had finally arrived, the truth of whether or not I had imagined the whole thing was about to be revealed. With a shaky breath I lead Liam over to the fallen wall opposite to where Jeremy had first spotted me and led me through the trees to his amusement park.

"So, I think you should hold my hand," I told Liam nervously. "I'm not sure if you'll find it if I don't lead you there." I was guessing that to find Jeremy's Amusement Park you had to be led there by someone who had been before. It had been Jeremy that had led me, and I was now going to lead Liam.

I bit my lip as his hand slid around mine, I could feel the hesitation in him and I feared that I was making a huge mistake. But we had gone too far to turn back; the only option was to go forward.

My legs felt weak as I lifted them one at a time and forced them forward. I held my eyes tightly closed as I entered the tree line. I took one step forward, careful not to trip on any wildlife I didn't know was there. Then I took another step, and another step and a few more steps, and then I began to worry about how many steps I had taken.

"What the…" Liam said from where he held my hand just a step behind me.

Slowly, I opened my eyes and let in the bright, flashing lights of Jeremy's Amusement Park. It was there. Liam's wide eyes and open mouth proved he could see it too and relief flooded through me, I wasn't crazy after all.

I hadn't realised how tightly Liam had been holding my hand until he released it and the bones seemed to move back into their original places. He took a few tentative steps forward; no words came from his open mouth but I could guess what he was thinking.

As Liam took in the extraordinary sight, I became aware of the ticket woman watching us from her table by the entrance and I realised if she knew we were there Jeremy would already know too.

If Jeremy knew I had actually managed to persuade Liam to the park he may have hidden from us, and if he had I doubted we would ever find him. Jeremy knew the ins and outs of the park a lot better than I did, that and given the fact that he could apparently conjure whatever he wanted from his mind, I knew that it would be almost impossible to locate him if he didn't want to be found.

"Come on," I told Liam, taking his now shaking hand once again and leading him to the entrance.

"Tickets," the woman said from her table. This time I didn't look at her or tell her why we were there, I walked past her without a word, desperately hoping that she wouldn't dispute the issue. Luckily, she didn't say another word to us as we left her table without buying or presenting a ticket.

Liam's star struck eyes glistened in the lights surrounding us and he turned his head from right to left taking in everything he could see, the rides, the games, the other visitors. He had stopped walking and as I pulled on his arm, I got a lesson on his muscle strength as he would not let me move him.

"We need to find Jeremy quickly," I begged him.

His head had stopped moving and he watched ahead of him, entranced by something. "Found him," Liam whispered as if too shocked to find his voice. Jeremy appeared to be unaware of our eyes on him as he talked happily to the man running the game he was playing.

Liam's rigid body didn't move and he didn't speak for a long while, he just remained standing absolutely still while he watched his brother who had died years ago playing at an Amusement Park he had created himself. Around us other visitors moved from place to place, not noticing or caring about our presence. I waited alongside Liam, unsure if I should speak or move or get Jeremy's attention, my head went from one brother to the other, waiting nervously for one of them to do something.

A deep hollow had taken over Liam's emerald eyes, as if they were no longer seeing what I was seeing. Seemingly forgetting my presence, he remained deep in shock as he waited motionlessly for Jeremy to notice him.

Jeremy's head finally turned, a casual smile lingered on his lips as his eyes scanned over us and then moved on across the rest of the park. Suddenly, his head snapped back in Liam's direction, his smile hesitated and then grew large, taking over both of his cheeks.

Anticipation held me in place as I waited to see what either of them would do. For what felt like an entire night and day they watched each other, it was like looking in some sort of distorted mirror. Both faces were similar but with several small differences that made them each stand out in their own way.

Jeremy's feet finally moved forward, slowly taking one step at a time until he was only a few feet away, both men kept their eyes locked together without a word.

"I can't believe this," Liam finally said. I had never noticed before but he was ever so slightly taller than his older brother, his face had matured past Jeremy's and now Liam appeared the older of the two.

"You've grown up a lot since I last saw you," Jeremy said, looking his brother up and down with approval and something else that I just couldn't figure out.

"It's been ten years," Liam said, his voice cracking as he spoke. A tear glistened from the corner of his eye. "I've missed you."

Jeremy didn't reply at first, until he lunged forward taking Liam in his arms. "I've missed you too."

A knot took a hold of my throat and I took a step away from the two brothers, allowing them to reunite without my interruption. In that moment the two brothers embraced, and the years they had been apart were wiped away.

"I'm sorry about this, Liam," Jeremy said, releasing his hold on his brother and turning away.

Liam furrowed his brows and opened his mouth as if to reply. Before he got the chance, we were both surrounded by the park's workers. Someone took a hold of both my arms and pulled them behind my back. I could feel rope being wrapped around my wrists. I tried to see who was tying me up but they held me tightly in place.

I looked to where Liam was in the same position; both the man from the Ferris wheel and water balloon booth had hold of him, tying his arms together. He was shouting for them to let him go, throwing his body around to get out of their grip but finally had to give in and stood still in front of them.

Somehow, all the visitors had disappeared and the park was empty other than its staff.

"What's going on?" I shouted at Jeremy. My plan had clearly not worked. Liam wasn't the answer I had been looking for and now we were both trapped at the park.

"What's going on," Jeremy said, looking too smug for my liking. "Is that neither of you will be leaving my park."

He nodded to the people behind us and they dragged us both away from Jeremy and down a path I recognized with a shiver down my spine. The cage.

"No!" I pulled my arms free from my captor and fell to ground from the force of his release. I barely had time to feel the ground graze my knees through my jeans before I was lifted to my feet again and pushed forward.

Before we made it to the lightless path leading to the cage, we took another turn I didn't recognise and were instead taken behind a row of vendor's tents. It was there we discovered another person, captured and tied up, sitting on the dirty ground with their legs crossed and head bent down.

"Mrs. Millar!" I gasped, as Liam and I were shoved to the ground next to her. I scooched closer to her prone form to see her eyes were closed but she was still breathing.

The workers-turned-guards stepped away but stayed close enough to keep an eye on us.

"Mrs. Millar." I pleaded for her attention. Slowly her eyes opened and her head lifted slowly toward me.

Her skin had taken on an ashy tone and she croaked as she spoke. "I won't be able to get you out of this one," she said.

"What are you doing here?" I asked, shock still shooting through my veins.

Mrs. Millar scoffed. "Well, it wasn't hard for Jeremy to work out how you had escaped. And he knew his conscience would only betray him again so he tied me up. Left me here to rot."

"Do you know what he's planning to do with us now?"

"No," she said. "But he has plans. I can tell something is in the works."

I sat back and only then remembered Liam's silent presence beside me. His face was the colour of a sheet of paper and his eyes were so wide it was as if he had seen a ghost. Which he had. His gaze was glued to the ground and he didn't appear to be moving at all.

"Liam?" I said, gently. He didn't speak at first and I said his name again.

"I can't believe it," he said so quietly I wasn't sure he had really spoken. "You were right. I thought you were mad. A raving lunatic. I was all set to prove you wrong tonight and recommend you get committed."

Well, it was nice to know how he really felt. I couldn't get too angry, seeing as I wasn't totally sure that I wasn't a raving lunatic myself.

"I think we're in real trouble here, Liam."

He looked up sharply. "Really? You think I thought being tied up by my dead brother, who hasn't aged in ten years, didn't suggest trouble for us?"

Mrs. Millar burst into a fit of dry coughs. "You should never have come back here."

"I thought we could help," I explained. "I thought he would move on when he saw Liam and this would all be over."

"Well, that didn't work, did it? What are you planning to do now?"

I took my defeat in silence and averted my eyes from both Mrs. Millar's and Liam's. I knew this was all my fault, I didn't need them to tell me that.

With the rope securely holding my arms together and three guards with their eyes on us, I had no solution to our problem. No solution to the problem I'd created. I searched every corner of my memory for anything else Jeremy had said that might indicate a way for him to let go and move on, but I couldn't think of anything.

Jeremy's figure appeared around the booth in front of us and he peered down his nose at his three prisoners. The blue of his eyes looked fierce.

"What do you want from us?" I asked.

"It's not what I want from you. It's what I want from my brother."

I looked to where Liam was glaring toward Jeremy. I couldn't even begin to imagine what he could be thinking.

"What do you mean?"

"It's quite simple actually. I figured it out when you said I couldn't stay here. You were right. I can't stay here forever. I knew it was only a matter of time until you came back and when you did, I planned to swap places with you. Your spirit would stay here and I would take your body and leave this place."

An icicle ran down my back. This couldn't be happening.

"But then I saw that you'd brought me something even better. My brother. My own flesh and blood. An almost perfect match for my own body. I could resume my life almost where it left off and no one would have to know. I could be a better me than I was the first time."

I had brought Liam here. This was all my fault.

"And how do you plan to take a body?"

"All I have to do is swap our souls." Jeremy looked at his brother who had been silent through this whole exchange.

I couldn't believe what I was hearing. It couldn't be possible.

"The plans are all in place. I was just waiting for your arrival. Soon, I will take over Liam's body and resume my life."

"And what about me? I'll tell someone, you won't get away with it," I threatened him.

"Who's going to believe you?" Jeremy looked down at his younger brother and for a moment I thought I saw regret in his eyes, but then he left us and we all sat in silence.

He was right, of course. Noone would believe me. I would be the local mad woman and no one would ever talk to me again. He would get away with it. Liam would lose his life and it would all be my fault. I had to do something. I twisted my arms where they were tied and pulled at them to get free, by the time I gave up I could feel the rope cutting into my skin.

"Mae," Liam said, eventually and I looked at him, shocked that he sounded so normal, so recognizable. Nothing else made sense, surely Liam was going to start changing on me too.

"Mae," he said again. "Something was weird about Jeremy. At first, he seemed like the old Jeremy but something changed in him when he hugged me. I don't think he's the same person anymore."

"Not the same person," I repeated. "Are you sure? It has been ten years."

"You think I don't know my own brother?" Liam snapped.

"No, I'm sure you do."

Not the same person, I said over and over in my mind until a flicker of light appeared.

"If he isn't the same person, then that must be why seeing you didn't have any effect on him," I said to no one in particular.

"Yes, that's kind of what I'm saying," Liam said.

"So," I continued, unsure of what exactly I was getting at. "Maybe we need to somehow bring the old Jeremy back."

"And how would we go about doing that?" Mrs. Millar piped up, suddenly interested in us again.

"I don't know exactly. We need to..." I searched hopelessly for an answer.

"We need to remind him of who he was," Liam said with confidence. "I need to remind him."

The three of us remained on the ground with our hands tied behind our back for a long time. When my thoughts eventually began to slow down, I noticed how quiet the park was without so many visitors. I could just about make out voices talking in the distance.

Careful not to attract the attention of the guards I scooched to the side of the stall we had been thrown behind and peered around the side. Jeremy was stood with a few other men a few stalls down from ours. His arms were crossed casually over his chest while the men all chatted.

There was no way I could get any closer to hear what they were talking about, but I was sure they had to be going over their plans to take Liam's body.

I had no idea how much time we had left to escape or create our own plan to bring the old Jeremy back, but I had a feeling it should be sooner rather than later.

The lack of sleep I'd had recently mixed toxically with my desperation to save Liam and before I knew what I was doing my mouth opened and I shouted to get Jeremy's attention. His head whipped round and his eyes met mine.

"Hey!" one of the guards shouted coming over to pull me back.

"What are you doing?" Liam hissed.

"Now's your chance to bring Jeremy back. Whatever you're planning you need to do it now," I whispered back so no one else would hear our plan.

Liam looked panicked when he looked to where Jeremy was approaching. He didn't look pleased at my interruption.

Before he could say anything, Liam took the chance to speak. "What do you want from us?"

Was that it? I wondered a little disappointed.

"I'll do whatever you want, Jeremy. Just don't do this." Liam pleaded. Jeremy looked a little embarrassed at Liam's attempt to sway his decision. "I'll come back every night to see you. We can hang out like we used to. Go on rides. It'll be just like the old days."

"What makes you think I want it to be just like the old days?" Jeremy smirked.

"Because I'm your brother," Liam said, a single tear forming at the corner of his eye.

"Unfortunately, Liam. That's just not good enough." Jeremy walked away.

"Liam, I-"

"It didn't work," Liam cut me off, turning his face away from mine.

"You're wrong," Mrs. Millar said from where she had just witnessed everything. We both turned to her for answers. "When Jeremy first appeared at this park, he used to talk about his life a lot, he talked about you a lot, Liam. After a while he stopped. I hadn't noticed it until you two arrived, but over time Jeremy changed."

We waited patiently for her to go on.

"Just then, when you were talking to him, I saw the Jeremy that arrived at this park ten years ago. I could see it in his face. He is there. Somewhere."

Hope sprang into my chest and I looked to Liam who didn't appear to be as hopeful as me. His eye had returned to his lap again. He slowly shook his head.

"No," he said. "I can't do anything else. That's all I had."

Quiet once again sat in the air between all three of us. There had to be something else we could do. Or maybe I could do it. I wanted desperately to help, not just Liam but myself.

My summer had started out perfectly normal, although maybe not the best. But my desperation to get over George had pushed me further toward Jeremy and then I had dragged Liam into this whole mess as well.

I remembered Liam telling me about how his life had somewhat turned around in the last few years. He had pushed himself toward the life he wanted, to make friends, get a job etc. I was sure I had ruined that all for him now. Even if, by some miracle, we did escape the park, I didn't know how Liam would get over the sight of his now evil dead brother trying to take his body.

Mrs. Millar seemed to have gone back to her old hateful self, like when I had first met her. She didn't seem particularly interested in actually helping other than the small amount she had already said.

It didn't really matter now, as if the plan was going to work it would have whether she warned him or not. And she did tell us that he seemed to go back to the old Jeremy, so maybe that meant she was on our side.

The one thing I knew was that I couldn't rely on her. Whatever happened next would be up to Liam and me.

In what felt like only minutes since Liam's interaction with Jeremy I began to notice the sky changing colour. Morning was coming. If we were still here when it became night again we would be missing from the real world for another whole day. I had no idea how I would explain that to my parents.

The guards came for us then, lifting us to our feet and pushing us round to the tent and back to the large empty space at the front of the park. Jeremy was waiting for us by himself, the rest of his workers were standing back at their stalls, just as they normally were, although their eyes remained on us.

The guards holding me and Mrs. Millar stopped at the edge of the row of game stalls and I watched as Liam was taken to Jeremy. The guards on either side of him stepped away, but left his hands tied together.

With his back hunched in defeat, Liam was no longer taller than Jeremy, he now appeared the same height, although still slightly thinner.

"Liam," Jeremy said with his signature grin. "Don't worry, this won't hurt. Probably."

"You don't have to go through with this. There's still time to release us," Liam said. Even I could hear that he didn't believe what he was saying.

Jeremy held his hand out to his side with his palm facing up and soon someone brought over a small pocket knife and planted it in his hand.

"To do this, we will have to drink each other's blood," Jeremy explained.

"I won't."

"You won't have a choice."

Jeremy took the knife and slid it carefully across Liam's neck as if he didn't really want to hurt him. Neither of them flinched. A deep red line appeared where the knife had been, as well as on the knife itself. I watched in horror as Jeremy held the knife above his head and a drop of blood fell into his mouth.

Then, Jeremy sliced the knife across his palm releasing enough blood to drip from his hand, then threw the knife to the ground. Two guards came over to hold Liam, one of them pushing his shoulders until his knees gave out and he knelt on the ground. The other guard put his hand around Liam's jaw and pulled it open so Jeremy could drop his blood into his brother's mouth.

While watching the horrible events taking place in front of us, my guard had loosened his grip and Mrs. Millar jumped sideways into him, knocking him a few long steps away.

"Go!" she shouted at me.

I took the opportunity, my hands still tied behind me, and dived forward towards the two brothers and their guards. They were all concentrating too hard on Jeremy and Liam to notice me jumping toward them. I shoved my body into the guard holding open Liam's mouth and we both fell to the ground before he could be made to drink his brother's blood. My whole left side ached with the force of my tackle but still I shuffled my body to stand, only for the guard to grab hold of me and throw me back down onto my stomach, placing his heavy foot on my back to hold me down.

Liam used his own body to shove Jeremy back and he landed on his back, his limbs sprayed out around him. He growled in anger.

The guard left beside Liam grabbed the knife from the ground and pulled Liam against his chest holding the knife against his neck.

"Jeremy, please," Liam begged.

Jeremy jumped up and rushed towards Liam, but halfway there it was as if someone had applied the brakes. He skidded to a stop, and his fierce eyes softened as he took in the sight in front of him.

"Liam?" Jeremy said as if confused. Then he shook his head and changed his tone back to the angry one it had been all night. "You thought you could escape?"

Jeremy was fighting his new self, I realised suddenly. It had been his old self that said Liam's name.

"He's there, Liam!" I shouted from where I was trapped on the ground. "Jeremy is still in there!"

Liam's eyes twitched to look at me and then straight back to his brother.

"Don't do this," he pleaded. "I'm your brother, Jeremy!"

The guard moved the knife closer to Liam's skin and a line of blood appeared slowly, seeping from beneath the blade.

"Help me," Liam whispered. "Remember me! I was twelve when you died, our parents didn't stop arguing after, for a long time it got worse. I couldn't walk for months; I was stuck in my bed listening to them all day and night."

"So what?" Jeremy said, looking slightly amused as he lifted himself off the ground.

"So, I needed you," Liam said, a single tear appearing at the corner of his eye. "I needed my big brother when the kids were making fun of me for limping in school. I need you when dad moved out and mum stopped leaving her room."

Jeremy's smirk had faded and he was watching Liam seriously.

"I needed you when my first girlfriend dumped me, and when my only friend changed schools. I needed my big brother!"

Jeremy stood straighter and swallowed, he didn't speak.

"Do you remember when I was a kid and you used to let me win on those skate boarding games we used to play, and I was so proud of myself for beating you? Or when we went out as a family and we used to go and explore the woodland while our parents stayed on the path and we would jump out and scare them? Do you even remember me at all?" Liam's chest deflated with his last questions and he lowered his eyes back down to his lap.

I'd never seen Liam this way. In the week that we had been spending time together we had barely talked about Jeremy at all, everything Liam had said had been quite factual, I had no idea how he was really feeling, what he had really been through.

A tear swam slowly down his cheek, dropped from his jaw and was soaked up by his shirt.

Jeremy took a step forward, looking intently at his brother. His eyes were now a deep blue colour. He put his hand on the wrist of the guard holding the knife.

"Stop," he said, as if unsure what he was saying. Then he looked up at the guard and said more sternly. "Stop."

The guard removed the knife and stepped back from Liam's body. Liam fell to the ground. He looked up at Jeremy who had his arm outstretched to hold him up.

Liam hesitated before allowing his brother to hook his hand under his arm and pull him up to standing.

"I'm so sorry, Liam," Jeremy said. "I never meant for this to happen."

Jeremy pulled Liam into an awkward hug, and I saw Liam's body go rigid at his touch.

"Perhaps you could untie him then?" I said.

Jeremy let go of him and went around him to untie the rope holding his hands together. He nodded at the guard whose foot was still holding me on the dirty ground and I was soon pulled to my feet and my hands released.

Liam watched his brother suspiciously.

"Liam, please listen to me," Jeremy begged, taking the hint and not coming any closer to his brother. "I don't know how long I have left. I need to apologise to you. For everything. For tonight. I don't know what happened to me, I was just so desperate to get out of here."

Liam looked like he was beginning to soften to his brother. "It's okay," he said.

"It's not okay. And I was a horrible brother when we were alive," Jeremy went on. "I should've treated you better." Around us I noticed the workers had disappeared. Only Mrs. Millar was left. She nodded at me, before she too disappeared into thin air.

"No," Liam said, suddenly stepping forward. "You were a good brother."

Jeremy shook his head as if he didn't agree but didn't want to say anything else on the matter.

"Liam, I just need to know one thing. Are you happy?"

"I am," Liam said, catching my eye as he said it. Jeremy saw the quick exchange and looked my way with a satisfied smile.

"Mae," Jeremy said. "I'm sorry for what I did to you. How I treated you. Please forgive me?"

"I do," I told him honestly.

The park itself became hard to see as it too began to disappear.

"This is it," Jeremy said.

"No!" Liam said suddenly. "You can't go. I have more to tell you. I need you."

Jeremy let out a slow breath and with it a kind smile grew on his face. "You don't need me anymore, Liam."

"I love you, Jeremy."

"I love you too. I'm so proud of you, Liam."

With those last words Jeremy was gone and we found ourselves looking over the old, abandoned amusement park where it had all started. We didn't speak to each other, we didn't move, we just stood in place.

"Liam," I said eventually, turning to see his tear-streaked face looking down at me. Without a word Liam took me in his arms and buried his face in my neck, heaving long breaths of despair. I held him to me as feelings I was sure he had been holding in for years overtook him. My heart broke as I felt Liam losing his brother for a second time, his pain soaking into the skin of my neck.

# Chapter 32

Liam didn't say a word to me during the whole walk back from the amusement park, but he kept a strong hold on my hand as I led his body through the forest and into town. Glittering stars no longer filled the dark sky, and I realised that this would be the last time I would be returning at daybreak, that I no longer had to bear the burden of Jeremy's pain, and the secret Amusement Park. It was over.

When I turned to face Liam for the first time since leaving the amusement park my heart broke all over again. The despair remained in red blotches over his skin but his eyes had taken on a hard shell as if a decision had been made in his head on the walk to my house. I knew something was about to end.

"I can't see you right now, Mae. I just need some time," he said, releasing my hand from his and turning away from me.

I had thought after that night Liam would forgive me and we could return to the way it had been before I had ever told him the truth about Jeremy, but now I knew nothing between us could be normal ever again.

-

Two weeks later I still hadn't heard from Liam. I'd spend that time focusing on infusing myself back into my friendship group, determined to stop myself from slipping back into the depression I had felt after my relationship with George had ended.

I had realised that Jeremy and Liam had both played a role in helping me get over my lingering feelings for George, and even if Liam never talked to me again at least I would know that something positive had come from everything that had happened. All I hoped was that Liam wasn't spiraling back into the dark place he had been in after losing Jeremy the first time.

My parents had claimed me on each of their days off work so we could spend precious time together before I was no longer living in the same house as them. Soon, I realised how much I had come to enjoy their company and how much I would miss them when I was no longer following their rules.

With only a few weeks until the day I moved into my university accommodation I kept my mind busy with planning and packing and shopping for anything else I would need, determined to ignore the thoughts I had about Liam, would I run into Liam when I was living in Lincoln? Would he remember that I was living only an hour away from him?

I told myself that I wouldn't see him and he wouldn't think of me and I would get on with my new life and he would get on with his life and it would be as if none of it had ever happened. And that was for the best, I tried to convince myself.

Then, two weeks after Liam and Jeremy had finally reconciled, I saw him. Dark, menacing clouds were quickly taking over the clear sky as I was preparing to meet up with my friends after a particularly hot day sun-bathing in my garden. I was rushing to get ready to go over to Jayne's house before what I knew would be a heavy downpour, when I heard a knock at the front door.

Glancing down from my bedroom window to see who it was I saw the top of a man's head that looked awfully like Liam's. Telling myself to stop being silly because why would he be outside the door of my house? I forced myself to go downstairs and answer the door.

The man stopped just as he was turning to leave.

"Liam?" I said as I caught sight of the side of his face. "What are you doing here?"

He stepped back up to the door. "Hi," he said with what looked like contained excitement when he saw me. His eyes travelled over my newly tanned skin, over my growing hair before hovering on my lips and finally landing on my eyes. "You're looking good. Really good."

"Thanks," I said, unable to stop my own grin from spreading across my face. I could barely believe my eyes, after two weeks of silence Liam was here in front of me. He didn't look mad, or sad or anything like I had expected.

"Mae, I'm sorry about not talking to you all this time," he said, taking a step closer and lifting my hands into his. "I completely understand if you don't want to talk to me. But I wanted to see if you were available for a coffee."

Relief flooded through me.

"I was just going to meet my friends," I told him and watched the disappointment swim over him. "Why don't you join us?"

Dear Reader,

Thank you so much for reading my book!

If you enjoyed it, please share with your friends and leave me a good review on Amazon and Instagram.

Don't forget to tag my Instagram k.t_Books

# ACKNOWLEDGEMENTS

First of all, I would like to thank my editor Kat Gordon for all of her amazing help. Without her this book would be completely different. I was able to find Kat through Reedsy.com.

Secondly, I would like to say a huge thank you to Serena for working with me to design the cover art.

Thank you to all of my friends and family who have always supported me to do what I love and have encouraged me to go after my dream.

Lastly, I would like to thank Lee, for his constant support in this book writing process and constant encouragement. As well as for reading hundreds of versions of the same story.

# About the Author

Katherine Taylor was raised in Cornwall where she still lives and works. As well as working full time she also posts book reviews on her Instagram account.

She has always loved creating stories and still has stacks of notebooks full of years' worth of writing.

This is Katherine's first novel and she can't wait to have people finally read it.

Printed in Great Britain
by Amazon

86637503R00149